Adeline Dutton Train Whitney

We Girls

A Home Story. 33rd Edition

Adeline Dutton Train Whitney

We Girls
A Home Story. 33rd Edition

ISBN/EAN: 9783744747080

Printed in Europe, USA, Canada, Australia, Japan

Cover: Foto ©Andreas Hilbeck / pixelio.de

More available books at **www.hansebooks.com**

BINDING THE RINGS.

WE GIRLS:

A HOME STORY.

BY

MRS. A. D. T. WHITNEY,

AUTHOR OF "FAITH GARTNEY'S GIRLHOOD," "THE GAYWORTHYS," "A SUMMER
IN LESLIE GOLDTHWAITE'S LIFE," ETC.

WITH ILLUSTRATIONS.

THIRTY-THIRD EDITION.

BOSTON:
HOUGHTON, MIFFLIN AND COMPANY.
New York: 11 East Seventeenth Street.
The Riverside Press, Cambridge.
1887.

CAMBRIDGE: PRINTED AT THE RIVERSIDE PRESS.

CONTENTS.

CHAPTER IX.

CHAPTER X.

CHAPTER XI.

CHAPTER XII.

WE GIRLS: A HOME STORY.

CHAPTER I.

THE STORY BEGINS.

T begins right in the middle; but a story must begin somewhere.

The town is down below the hill.

It lies in the hollow, and stretches on till it runs against another hill, over opposite; up which it goes a little way before it can stop itself, just as it does on this side.

It is no matter for the name of the town. It is a good, large country town, — in fact, it has some time since come under city regulations, — thinking sufficiently well of itself, and, for that which it lacks, only twenty miles from the metropolis.

Up our hill straggle the more ambitious houses, that have shaken off the dust from their feet, or their founda-

1

tions, and surrounded themselves with green grass, and
are shaded with trees, and are called "places." There
are the Marchbanks places, and the "Haddens," and the
old Pennington place.   At these houses they dine at five
o'clock, when the great city bankers and merchants come
home in the afternoon train ; down in the town, where
people keep shops, or doctors' or lawyers' offices, or manage the Bank, and where the manufactories are, they eat
at one, and have long afternoons ; and the schools keep
twice a day.

   We lived in the town — that is, Mr. and Mrs. Holabird
did, and their children, for such length of the time as their
ages allowed — for nineteen years ; and then we moved
to Westover, and this story began.

   They called it "Westover," more or less, years and
years before ; when there were no houses up the hill at
all ; only farm lands and pastures, and a turnpike road
running straight up one side and down the other, in the
sun.   When anybody had need to climb over the crown,
to get to the fields on this side, they called it "going west
over" ; and so came the name.

   We always thought it was a pretty, sunsetty name ;
but it is n't considered quite so fine to have a house here
as to have it below the brow.   When you get up sufficiently high, in any sense, you begin to go down again.
Or is it that people can't be distinctively genteel, if they
get so far away from the common as no longer to well
overlook it ?

   Grandfather Holabird — old Mr. Rufus, — I don't say
whether he was my grandfather or not, for it does n't
matter which Holabird tells this story, or whether it is a

Holabird at all — bought land here ever so many years ago, and built a large, plain, roomy house; and here the boys grew up, — Roderick and Rufus and Stephen and John.

Roderick went into the manufactory with his father, — who had himself come up from being a workman to being owner, — and learned the business, and made money, and married a Miss Bragdowne from C——, and lived on at home. Rufus married and went away, and died when he was yet a young man. His wife went home to her family, and there were no little children. John lives in New York, and has two sons and three daughters.

There are of us — Stephen Holabird's family — just six. Stephen and his wife, Rosamond and Barbara and little Stephen and Ruth. Ruth is Mrs. Holabird's niece, and Mr. Holabird's second cousin; for two cousins married two sisters. She came here when she had neither father nor mother left. They thought it queer up at the other house; because "Stephen had never managed to have any too much for his own"; but of course, being the wife's niece, they never thought of interfering, on the mere claim of the common cousinship.

Ruth Holabird is a quiet little body, but she has her own particular ways too.

There is one thing different in our house from most others. We are all known by our straight names. I say *known;* because we do have little pet ways of calling, among ourselves, — sometimes one way and sometimes another; but we don't let these get out of doors much. Mr. Holabird does n't like it. So though up stairs, over our sewing, or our bed-making, or our dressing, we shorten

or sweeten, or make a little fun, — though Rose of the
world gets translated, if she looks or behaves rather spe-
cially nice, or stays at the glass trying to do the first, — or
Barbara gets only " Barb " when she is sharper than common, or Stephen is "Steve" when he's a dear, and
" Stiff" when he's obstinate, — we always *introduce* "my
daughter Rosamond," or " my sister Barbara," or, — but
Ruth of course never gets nicknamed, because nothing
could be easier or pleasanter than just " Ruth," — and
Stephen is plain strong Stephen, because he is a boy and
is expected to be a man some time. Nobody writes to us,
or speaks of us, except as we were christened. This is
only rather a pity for Rosamond. Rose Holabird is such a
pretty name. " But it will keep," her mother tells her.
" She would n't want to be everybody's Rose."

Our moving to Westover was a great time.

That was because we had to move the house ; which is
what everybody does not do who moves into a house by
any means.

We were very much astonished when Grandfather
Holabird came in and told us, one morning, of his having
bought it, — the empty Beaman house, that nobody had
lived in for five years. The Haddens had bought the
land for somebody in their family who wanted to come out
and build, and so the old house was to be sold and moved
away ; and nobody but old Mr. Holabird owned land near
enough to put it upon. For it was large and solid-built,
and could not be taken far.

We were a great deal more astonished when he came
in again, another day, and proposed that we should go and
live in it.

We were all a good deal afraid of Grandfather Holabird. He had very strict ideas of what people ought to do about money. Or rather of what they ought to do *without* it, when they did n't happen to have any.

Mrs. Stephen pulled down the green blinds when she saw him coming that day, — him and his cane. Barbara said she did n't exactly know which it was she dreaded; she thought she could bear the cane without him, or even him without the cane; but both together were "*scaremendous*; they did put down so."

Mrs. Holabird pulled down the blinds, because he would be sure to notice the new carpet the first thing; it was a cheap ingrain, and the old one had been all holes, so that Barbara had proposed putting up a board at the door, — "Private way; dangerous passing." And we had all made over our three winters' old cloaks this year, for the sake of it: and we had n't got the carpet then till the winter was half over. But we could n't tell all this to Grandfather Holabird. There was never time for the whole of it. And he knew that Mr. Stephen was troubled just now for his rent and taxes. For Stephen Holabird was the one in this family who could n't make, or could n't manage, money. There is always one. I don't know but it is usually the best one of all, in other ways.

Stephen Holabird is a good man, kind and true; loving to live a gentle, thoughtful life, in his home and among his books; not made for the din and scramble of business.

He never looks to his father; his father does not believe in allowing his sons to look to him; so in the terrible time of '57, when the loss and the worry came, he had to struggle as long as he could, and then go down with the rest, paying sixty cents on the dollar of all his debts, and beginning again, to try and earn the forty, and to feed and clothe his family meanwhile.

Grandfather Holabird sent us down all our milk, and once a week, when he bought his Sunday dinner, he would order a turkey for us. In the summer, we had all the vegetables we wanted from his garden, and at Thanksgiving a barrel of cranberries from his meadow. But these obliged us to buy an extra half-barrel of sugar. For all these things we made separate small change of thanks, each time, and were all the more afraid of his noticing our new gowns or carpets.

" When you have n't any money, don't buy anything," was his stern precept.

" When you 're in the Black Hole, don't breathe," Barbara would say, after he was gone.

But then we thought a good deal of Grandfather Holabird, for all. That day, when he came in and astonished us so, we were all as busy and as cosey as we could be.

Mrs. Holabird was making a rug of the piece of the new carpet that had been cut out for the hearth, bordering it with a strip of shag. Rosamond was inventing a feather for her hat out of the best of an old black-cock plume, and some bits of beautiful downy white ones with smooth tips, that she brought forth out of a box.

" What are they, Rose ? And where did you get them ? " Ruth asked, wondering.

" They were dropped, — and I picked them up," Rosamond answered, mysteriously. " The owner never missed them."

" Why, Rosamond ! " cried Stephen, looking up from his Latin grammar.

"Did!" persisted Rosamond. "And would again. I'm sure I wanted 'em most. Hens lay themselves out on their underclothing, don't they?" she went on, quietly, putting the white against the black, and admiring the effect. "They don't dress much outside."

"O, hens! What did you make us think it was people for?"

"Don't you ever let anybody know it was hens! Never cackle about contrivances. Things must n't be contrived; they must happen. Woman and her accidents, — mine are usually catastrophes."

Rosamond was so busy fastening in the plume, and giving it the right set-up, that she talked a little delirium of nonsense.

Barbara flung down a magazine, — some old number. "Just as they were putting the very tassel on to the cap of the climax, the page is torn out! What do you want, little cat?" she went on to her pussy, that had tumbled out of her lap as she got up, and was stretching and mewing. "Want to go out doors and play, little cat? Well, you can. There's plenty of room out of doors for two little cats!" And going to the door with her, she met grandfather and the cane coming in.

There was time enough for Mrs. Holabird to pull down the blinds, and for Ruth to take a long, thinking look out from under hers, through the sash of window left unshaded; for old Mr. Holabird and his cane were slow; the more awful for that.

Ruth thought to herself, "Yes; there is plenty of room out of doors; and yet people crowd so! I wonder why we can't live bigger!"

Mrs. Holabird's thinking was something like it.

"Five hundred dollars to worry about, for what is set down upon a few square yards of ' out of doors.' And inside of that, a great contriving and going without, to put something warm underfoot over the sixteen square feet that we live on most!"

She had almost a mind to pull up the blinds again; it was such a very little matter, the bit of new carpet, after all.

"How do I know what they were thinking?" Never mind. People do know, or else how do they ever tell stories? We know lots of things that we *don't* tell all the time. We don't stop to think whether we know them or not; but they are underneath the things we feel, and the things we do.

Grandfather came in, and said over the same old stereotypes. He had a way of saying them, so that we knew just what was coming, sentence after sentence. It was a kind of family psalter. What it all meant was, "I've looked in to see you, and how you are getting along. I do think of you once in a while." And our worn-out responses were, " It 's very good of you, and we 're much obliged to you, as far as it goes."

It was only just as he got up to leave that he said the real thing. When there was one, he always kept it to the last.

" Your lease is up here in May, is n't it, Mrs. Stephen ? "

" Yes, sir."

" I 'm going to move over that Beaman house next month, as soon as the ground settles. I thought it might suit you, perhaps, to come and live in it. It would be handier about a good many things than it is now. Stephen might do something to his piece, in a way of small farming. I 'd let him have the rent for three years. You can talk it over."

He turned round and walked right out. Nobody thanked him or said a word. We were too much surprised.

Mother spoke first; after we had hushed up Stephen, who shouted.

I shall call her " mother," now; for it always seems as if that were a woman's real name among her children. Mr. Holabird was apt to call her so himself. She did not altogether like it, always, from him. She asked him once if "Emily" were dead and buried. She had tried to keep her name herself, she said; that was the reason she had not given it to either of her daughters. It was a good thing to leave to a grandchild; but she could not do without it as long as she lived.

"We could keep a cow!" said mother.

"We could have a pony!" cried Stephen, utterly disregarded.

"What does he want to move it quite over for?" asked Rosamond. "His land begins this side."

"Rosamond wants so to get among the Hill people! Pray, why can't we have a colony of our own?" said Barbara, sharply and proudly.

"I should think it would be less trouble," said Rosamond, quietly, in continuation of her own remark; holding up, as she spoke, her finished hat upon her hand. Rosamond aimed at being truly elegant. She would never discuss, directly, any questions of our position, or our limitations.

"Does that look —"

"Holabirdy?" put in Barbara. "No. Not a bit. Things that you do never do."

Rosamond felt herself flush up. Alice Marchbanks had said once, of something that we wore, which was praised as pretty, that it "might be, but it was Holabirdy." Rosamond found it hard to forget that.

"I beg your pardon, Rose. It 's just as pretty as it can be; and I don't mean to tease you," said Barbara, quickly. "But I *do* mean to be proud of being Holabirdy, just as long as there 's a piece of the name left."

I wish we had n't bought the new carpet now," said mother. "And what *shall* we do about all those other great rooms? It will take ready money to move. I 'm afraid we shall have to cut it off somewhere else for a while. What if it should be the music, Ruth?"

That did go to Ruth's heart. She tried so hard to be willing that she did not speak at first.

"'Open and shet is a sign of more wet!'" cried Barbara. "I don't believe there ever was a family that had so *much* opening and shetting! We just get a little squeak out of a crack, and it goes together again and snips our noses!"

"What *is* a 'squeak' out of a crack?" said Rosamond, laughing. "A mouse pinched in it, I should think."

"Exactly," replied Barbara. "The most expressive words are fricassees, — heads and tails dished up together. Can't you see the philology of it? 'Squint' and 'peek.' Worcester can't put down everything. He leaves something to human ingenuity. The language is n't all made, — or used, — yet!"

Barbara had a way of putting heads and tails together, in defiance — in aid, as she maintained — of the dictionaries.

"O, I can practise," Ruth said, cheerily. "It will be so bright out there, and the mornings will be so early!"

"That 's just what they won't be, particularly," said Barbara, "seeing we 're going 'west over.'"

"Well, then, the afternoons will be long. It is all the same," said Ruth. That was the best she could do.

"Mother," said Rosamond, "I 've been thinking. Get grandfather to have some of the floors stained. I think rugs, and English druggets, put down **with** brass-headed nails, in the middle, are delightful. Especially for a country **try** house.''

" **It seems,** then, **we** *are* going ? "

Nobody had even raised a question of that.

Nobody raised a question when Mr. Holabird came in. He himself raised none. **He sat and** listened to all the propositions and corollaries, quite as one **does go** through the form of demonstration of a geometrical fact **patent at** first glance.

" We can have **a** cow," mother repeated.

" **Or a dog, at any rate,"** put in Stephen, who found **it** hard **to** get a hearing.

" You can have a garden, father," **said** Barbara. " It 's **to** be near to the **parcel of ground** that Rufus **gave** to his son Stephen."

"I don't **like** to have **you quote** Scripture so," **said** father, gravely.

"I don't," said Barbara. " **It** quoted **itself.** And **it** is n't there either. I don't **know of a** Rufus in all sacred history. **And there are n't** many in profane."

" Somebody was the ' father of Alexander and Rufus '; and there 's a Rufus ' saluted ' at the end **of an** epistle."

" Ruth is **sure to** catch one, if one 's out in Scripture. But that is n't history ; that 's mere mention."

" We can ask the girls to come ' over ' now, instead **of** ' down,' " suggested Rosamond, complacently.

Barbara smiled.

" And we **can tell** *the girl* to come ' over,' instead of ' up,' when she 's **to** fetch us home from a tea-drinking. That **will** be one of the ' handy ' things."

"Girl! we shall have a man, if we have a garden."
This was between the two.

"Mayhap," said Barbara. "And perlikely a wheel-barrow."

"We shall all have to remember that it will only be living there instead of here," said father, cautiously, putting up an umbrella under the rain of suggestion.

The umbrella settled the question of the weather, however. There was no doubt about it after that. Mother calculated measurements, and it was found out, between her and the girls, that the six muslin curtains in our double town parlor would be lovely for the six windows in the square Beaman best room. Also that the parlor carpet would make over, and leave pieces for rugs for some of our delightful stained floors. The little tables, and the two or three brackets, and the few pictures, and other art-ornaments, that only "strinkled," Barbara said, in two rooms, would be charmingly "crowsy" in one. And up stairs there would be such nice space for cushioning and flouncing, and making upholstery out of nothing, that you could n't do here, because in these spyglass houses the sleeping-rooms were all bedstead, and fireplace, and closet doors.

They were left to their uninterrupted feminine speculations, for Mr. Holabird had put on his hat and coat again, and gone off west over to see his father; and Stephen had "piled" out into the kitchen, to communicate his delight to Winifred, with whom he was on terms of a kind of odd-glove intimacy, neither of them having in the house any precisely matched companionship.

This ought to have been foreseen, and an embargo put

on ; for it led to trouble. By the time the green holland shades were apportioned to their new places, and an approximate estimate reached of the whole number of windows to be provided, Winny had made up her gregarious mind that she could not give up her town connection, and go out to live in " sûch a fersaakunness "; and as any remainder of time is to Irish valuation like the broken change of a dollar, when the whole can no longer be counted on, she gave us warning next morning at breakfast that she " must jûst be lukkin out fer a plaashe."

" But," said mother, in her most conciliatory way, " it must be two or three months, Winny, before we move, if we do go; and I should be glad to have you stay and help us through."

" Ah, sure, I 'd do annything to hilp yiz through ; an' I 'm sure, I taks an intheresht in yiz ahl, down to the little cat hersel' ; an' indeed I niver tuk an intheresht in anny little cat but that little cat ; but I could n't go live where it wud be so loahnsome, an' I can't be out oo a plaashe, ye see."

It was no use talking ; it was only transposing sentences ; she " tuk a graat intheresht in us, an' sure she 'd do annything to hilp us, but she mûst jûst be lukkin out fer hersel'." And that very day she had the kitchen scrubbed up at a most unwonted hour, and her best bonnet on, — a rim of flowers and lace, with a wide expanse of ungarnished head between it and the chignon it was supposed to accommodate, — and took her " afternoon out " to search for some new situation, where people were subject neither to sickness nor removals nor company nor children nor much of anything ; and where, under these circumstances, and especially if there were " set tubs, and hot and cold water," she would probably remain just about as long as her " intheresht " would *not* allow of her continuing with us.

A kitchen exodus is like other small natural commotions, — sure to happen when anything greater does. When the sun crosses the line we have a gale down below.

" *Now* what shall we do ? " asked Mrs. Holabird, forlornly, coming back into the sitting-room out of that vacancy in the farther apartments which spreads itself in such a still desertedness of feeling all through the house.

" Just what we 've done before, motherums ! " said Barbara, more bravely than she felt. " The next one is somewhere. Like Tupper's ' wife of thy youth,' she must be ' now living upon the earth.' In fact, I don't doubt there 's a long line of them yet, threaded in and out among the rest of humanity, all with faces set by fate toward our back door. There 's always a coming woman, in that direction at least."

" I would as lief come across the staying one," said Mrs. Holabird, with meekness.

It cooled down our enthusiasm. Stephen, especially, was very much quenched.

The next one was not only somewhere, but everywhere, it seemed, and nowhere. " Everything by turns and nothing long," Barbara wrote up over the kitchen chimney with the baker's chalk. We had five girls between that time and our moving to Westover, and we had to move without a girl at last; only getting a woman in to do days' work. But I have not come to the family-moving yet.

The house-moving was the pretty part. Every pleasant afternoon, while the building was upon the rollers, we walked over, and went up into all the rooms, and looked out of every window, noting what new pictures they gave as the position changed from day to day; how now this tree and now that shaded them: how we gradually came to see by the end of the Haddens' barn, and at last across it, — for the slope, though gradual, was long, — and how the sunset came in more and more, as we squared toward the west; and there was always a thrill of excitement when we felt under us, as we did again and again, the onward momentary surge of the timbers, as the workmen brought all rightly to bear, and the great team of oxen started up. Stephen called these earthquakes.

We found places, day by day, where it would be nice to stop. It was such a funny thing to travel along in a house that might stop anywhere, and thenceforward belong. Only, in fact, it could n't; because, like some other things that seem a matter of choice, it was all preordained; and there was a solid stone foundation waiting over on the west side, where grandfather meant it to be.

We got little new peeps at the southerly hills, in the fresh breaks between trees and buildings that we went by. As we reached the broad, open crown, we saw away down beyond where it was still and woodsy; and the nice farm-fields of Grandfather Holabird's place looked sunny and pleasant and real countrified.

It was not a steep eminence on either side; if it had been the great house could not have been carried over as it was. It was a grand generous swell of land, lifting up with a slow serenity into pure airs and splendid vision.

We did not know, exactly, where the highest point had been; but as we came on toward the little walled-in excavation which seemed such a small mark to aim at, and one which we might so easily fail to hit after all, we saw how behind us rose the green bosom of the field against the sky, and how, day by day, we got less of the great town within our view as we settled down upon our side of the ridge.

The air was different here; it was full of hill and pasture.

There were not many trees immediately about the spot where we were to be; but a great group of ashes and walnuts stood a little way down against the roadside, and all around in the far margins of the fields were beautiful elms, and round maples that would be globes of fire in autumn days, and above was the high blue glory of the unobstructed sky.

The ground fell off suddenly into a great hill-dimple, just where the walls were laid; that was why Grandfather Holabird had chosen the spot. There could be a cellar-kitchen; and it had been needful for the moving, that all the rambling, outrunning L, which had held the kitchens and woodsheds before, should be cut off and disposed of as mere lumber. It was only the main building — L-shaped still, of three very large rooms below and five by more subdivision above — which had majestically taken up its line of march, like the star of empire, westward. All else that was needful must be rebuilt.

Mother did not like a cellar-kitchen. It would be inconvenient with one servant. But Grandfather Holabird had planned the house before he offered it to us to live in.

2

What we were going to save in rent we must take out cheerfully in extra steps.

It was in the bright, lengthening days of April, when the bluebirds came fluttering out of fairy-land, that the old house finally stopped, and stood staring around it with its many eyes, — wide open to the daylight, all its green winkers having been taken off, — to see where it was and was likely to be for the rest of its days. It had a very knowing look, we thought, like a house that had seen the world.

The sun walked round it graciously, if not inquisitively. He flashed in at the wide parlor windows and the rooms overhead, as soon as he got his brow above the hill-top. Then he seemed to sidle round southward, not slanting wholly out his morning cheeriness until the noonday glory slanted in. At the same time he began with the sitting-room opposite, through the one window behind ; and then through the long, glowing afternoon, the whole bright west let him in along the full length of the house, till he just turned the last corner, and peeped in, on the longest summer days, at the very front. This was what he had got so far as to do by the time we moved in, — as if he stretched his very neck to find out the last there was to learn about it, and whether nowhere in it were really yet any human life. He quieted down in his mind, I suppose, when from morning to night he found somebody to beam at, and a busy doing in every room. He took it serenely then, as one of the established things upon the earth, and put us in the regular list of homes upon his round, that he was to leave so many cubic feet of light at daily.

I think he might like to look in at that best parlor.

With the six snowy-curtained windows, it was like a great white blossom ; and the deep-green carpet and the walls with vine-leaves running all over them, in the graceful-patterned paper that Rosamond chose, were like the moss and foliage among which it sprung. Here and there the light glinted upon gilded frame or rich bronze or pure Parian, and threw out the lovely high tints, and deepened the shadowy effects, of our few fine pictures. We had little of art, but that little was choice. It was Mr. Holabird's weakness, when money was easy with him, to bring home straws like these to the home nest. So we had, also, a good many nice books ; for, one at a time, when there was no hurrying bill to be paid, they had not seemed much to buy ; and in our brown room, where we sat every day, and where our ivies had kindly wonted themselves already to the broad, bright windows, there were stands and cases well filled, and a great round family table in the middle, whose worn cloth hid its shab-biness under the comfort of delicious volumes ready to the hand, among which, central of all, stood the Shekinah of the home-spirit, — a tall, large-globed lamp that drew us cosily into its round of radiance every night.

Not these June nights though. I will tell you presently what the June nights were at Westover.

We worked hard in those days, but we were right blithe about it. We had at last got an Irish girl from "far down,"— that is their word for the north country at home. and the north country is where the best material comes from, — who was willing to air her ignorance in our kitchen, and try our Christian patience, during a long pupilage, for the modest sum of three dollars a week ; than which

" she could not come indeed for less," said the friend who
brought her. " All the girls was gettin' that." She had
never seen dipped toast, and she " could n't do starched
clothes very skilful "; but these things had nothing to do
with established rates of wages.

But who cared, when it was June, and the smell of
green grass and the singing of birds were in the air, and
everything indoors was clean, and fresh with the wonderful freshness of things set every one in a new place? We
worked hard and we made it look lovely, if the things
were old ; and every now and then we stopped in the
midst of a busy rush, at door or window, to see joyfully
and exclaim with ecstasy how grandly and exquisitely
Nature was furbishing up her beautiful old things also,—
a million for one sweet touches outside, for ours in.

" Westover is no longer an adverbial phrase, even qual-
ifying the verb ' to go,' " said Barbara, exultingly, looking
abroad upon the family settlement, to which our new barn,
rising up, added another building. " It is an undoubted
substantive proper, and takes a preposition before it, except
when it is in the nominative case."

Because of the cellar-kitchen, there was a high piazza
built up to the sitting-room windows on the west, which
gradually came to the ground-level along the front. Under this was the woodshed. The piazza was open, unroofed : only at the front door was a wide covered portico,
from which steps went down to the gravelled entrance.
A light low railing ran around the whole.

Here we had those blessed country hours of day-done,
when it was right and lawful to be openly idle in this
world, and to look over through the beautiful evening

glooms to neighbor worlds, that showed always a round of busy light, and yet seemed somehow to keep holiday-time with us, and to be only out at play in the spacious ether.

We used to think of the sunset all the day through, wondering what new glory it would spread for us, and gathering eagerly to see, as for the witnessing of a pageant.

The moon was young, for our first delight; and the evening planet hung close by; they dropped down through

the gold together, till they touched the very rim of the farthest possible horizon; when they slid silently beneath, we caught our suspended breath.

"But the curtain is n't down," said Barbara, after a hush.

No.   The great scene was all open, still.   Wide from
north to south stretched the deep, sweet heaven, full of
the tenderest tints and softliest creeping shadows ; the
tree-fringes stood up against it ; the gentle winds swept
through, as if creatures winged, invisible, went by ;
touched, one by one, with glory, the stars burned on the
blue ; we watched as if any new, unheard-of wonder might
appear ; we looked out into great depths that narrow daylight shut us in from.   Daylight was the curtain.

"We've got the best balcony seats, have n't we,
father ? " Barbara said again, coming to where Mr.
Holabird sat, and leaning against the railing.

"The front row, and season tickets ! "

"Every one, all summer.   Only think ! " said Ruth.

"Pho !   You 'll get used to it," answered Stephen, as
if he knew human nature, and had got used himself to
most things.

CHAPTER II.

AMPHIBIOUS.

HAT day of the month is it?" asked Mrs. Holabird, looking up from her letter.

Ruth told.

"How do you always know the day of the month?" said Rosamond. "You are as pat as the almanac. I have to stop and think whether anything particular has happened, to remember *any* day by, since the first, and then count up. So, as things don't happen much out here, I 'm never sure of anything except that it can't be more than the thirty-first; and as to whether it can be that, I have to say over the old rhyme in my head."

"I know how she tells," spoke up Stephen. "It 's that thing up in her room, — that pious thing that whops over. It has the figures down at the bottom; and she whops it every morning."

Ruth laughed.

" What do you try to tease her for ? " said Mrs. Holabird.

" It does n't tease her. She thinks it 's funny. She
laughed, and you only puckered."

Ruth laughed again. " It was n't only that," she
said.

" Well, what then ? "

" To think you knew."

" Knew ! Why should n't I know ? It 's big enough."

" Yes, — but about the whopping. And the figures
are the smallest part of the difference. You 're a pretty
noticing boy, Steve."

Steve colored a little, and his eye twinkled. He saw
that Ruth had caught him out.

" I guess you set it for a goody-trap," he said. " Folks
can't help reading sign-boards when they go by. And
besides, it 's like the man that went to Van Amburgh's.
I shall catch you forgetting, some fine day, and then I 'll
whop the whole over for you."

Ruth had been mending stockings, and was just folding
up the last pair. She did not say any more, for she did
not want to tease Stephen in her turn : but there was a
little quiet smile just under her lips that she kept from
pulling too hard at the corners, as she got up and went
away with them to her room.

She stopped when she got to the open door of it, with
her basket in her hand, and looked in from the threshold
at the hanging scroll of Scripture texts printed in large
clear letters, — a sheet for each day of the month, — and
made to fold over and drop behind the black-walnut rod
to which they were bound. It had been given her by

her teacher at the Bible Class, — Mrs. Ingleside ; and Ruth loved Mrs. Ingleside very much.

Then she went to her bureau, and put her stockings in their drawer, and set the little basket, with its cotton-ball and darner, and maplewood egg, and small sharp scissors, on the top ; and then she went and sat down by the window, in her white considering-chair.

For she had something to think about this morning.

Ruth's room had three doors. It was the middle room up stairs, in the beginning of the L. Mrs. Holabird's opened into it from the front, and just opposite her door another led into the large, light corner room at the end, which Rosamond and Barbara occupied. Stephen's was on the other side of the three-feet passage which led straight through from the front staircase to the back of the house. The front staircase was a broad, low-stepped, old-fashioned one, with a landing half-way up ; and it was from this landing that a branch half-flight came into the L, between these two smaller bedrooms. Now I have begun, I may as well tell you all about it ; for, if you are like me, you will be glad to be taken fairly into a house you are to pay a visit in, and find out all the pleasant-nesses of it, and whom they especially belong to.

Ruth's room was longest across the house, and Stephen's with it ; behind his was only the space taken by some closets and the square of staircase beyond. This staircase had landings also, and was lighted by a window high up in the wall. Behind Ruth's, as I have said, was the whole depth of a large apartment. But as the passage divided the L unequally, it gave the rooms similar space and shape, only at right angles to each other.

The sun came into Stephen's room in the morning, and
into Ruth's in the afternoon; in the middle of the day the
passage was one long shine, from its south window at the
end, right through, — except in such days as these, that
were too deep in the summer to bear it, and then the
green blinds were shut all around, and the warm wind
drew through pleasantly in a soft shade.

When we brought our furniture from the house in the
town, the large front rooms and the open halls used it up
so, that it seemed as if there were hardly anything left
but bedsteads and washstands and bureaus, — the very
things that make up-stairs look so *very* bedroomy.   And
we wanted pretty places to sit in, as girls always do.   Rosamond and Barbara made a box-sofa, fitted luxuriously
with old pew-cushions sewed together, and a crib mattress
cut in two and fashioned into seat and pillows; and a
packing-case dressing-table, flounced with a skirt of white
cross-barred muslin that Ruth had outgrown.   In ex-
change for this Ruth bargained for the dimity curtains
that had furnished their two windows before, and would
not do for the three they had now.

Then she shut herself up one day in her room, and
made them all go round by the hall and passage, back and
forth; and worked away mysteriously till the middle of
the afternoon, when she unfastened all the doors again
and set them wide, as they have for the most part remained ever since, in the daytimes; thus rendering Ruth's
doings and ways particularly patent to the household, and
most conveniently open to the privilege and second sight
of story-telling.

The white dimity curtains — one pair of them — were

up at the wide west window; the other pair was cut up and made over into three or four things, — drapery for a little old pine table that had come to light among attic lumber, upon which she had tacked it in neat plaitings around the sides, and overlapped it at the top with a plain hemmed cover of the same; a great discarded toilet-cushion freshly encased with more of it, and edged with magic ruffling; the stained top and tied-up leg of a little disabled teapoy, kindly disguised in uniform, — varied only with a narrow stripe of chintz trimming in crimson arabesque, — made pretty with piles of books, and the Scripture scroll hung above it with its crimson cord and tassels; and in the window what she called afterward her "considering-chair," and in which she sat this morning; another antique, clothed purely from head to foot and made comfortable beneath with stout bagging nailed across, over the deficient cane-work.

Tin tacks and some considerable machining — for mother had lent her the help of her little "common sense" awhile — had done it all; and Ruth's room, with its oblong of carpet, — which Mrs. Holabird and she had made out before, from the brightest breadths of her old dove-colored one and a bordering of crimson venetian, of which there had not been enough to put upon the staircase, — looked, as Barbara said, "just as if it had been done on purpose."

"It *says* it all, anyhow, does n't it?" said Ruth.

Ruth was delightedly satisfied with it, — with its situation above all; she liked to nestle in, in the midst of people; and she never minded their coming through, any more than they minded her slipping her three little brass bolts when she had a desire to.

She sat down in her considering-chair to-day, to think about Adelaide Marchbanks's invitation.

The two Marchbanks houses were very gay this summer. The married daughter of one family — Mrs. Reyburne — was at home from New York, and had brought a very fascinating young Mrs. Van Alstyne with her. Roger Marchbanks, at the other house, had a couple of college friends visiting him; and both places were merry with young girls, — several sisters in each family, — always. The Haddens were there a good deal, and there were people from the city frequently, for a few days at a time. Mrs. Linceford was staying at the Haddens, and Leslie Goldthwaite, a great pet of hers, — Mr. Aaron Goldthwaite's daughter, in the town, — was often up among them all.

The Holabirds were asked in to tea-drinkings, and to croquet, now and then, especially at the Haddens', whom they knew best; but they were not on "in and out" terms, from morning to night, as these others were among themselves; for one thing, the little daily duties of their life would not allow it. The "jolly times" on the Hill were a kind of Elf-land to them, sometimes patent and free, sometimes shrouded in the impalpable and impassable mist that shuts in the fairy region when it wills to be by itself for a time.

There was one little simple sesame which had a power this way for them, perhaps without their thinking of it; certainly it was not spoken of directly when the invitations were given and accepted. Ruth's fingers had a little easy, gladsome knack at music; and I suppose sometimes it was only Ruth herself who realized how thorough-

ly the fingers earned the privilege of the rest of her bodily
presence. She did not mind; she was as happy playing
as Rosamond and Barbara dancing; it was all fair enough;
everybody must be wanted for something; and Ruth
knew that her music was her best thing. She wished
and meant it to be; Ruth had plans in her head which
her fingers were to carry out.

But sometimes there was a slight flavor in attention,
that was not quite palatable, even to Ruth's pride. These
three girls had each her own sort of dignity. Rosamond's
measured itself a good deal by the accepted dignity of
others; Barbara's insisted on its own standard; why
should n't they — the Holabirds — settle anything? Ruth
hated to have theirs hurt; and she did not like subservi-
ency, or courting favor. So this morning she was partly
disturbed and partly puzzled by what had happened.

Adelaide Marchbanks had overtaken her on the hill, on
her way "down street" to do some errand, and had
walked on with her very affably. At parting she had
said to her, in an off-hand, by-the-way fashion, —

"Ruth, why won't you come over to-night, and take
tea? I should like you to hear Mrs. Van Alstyne sing,
and she would like your playing. There won't be any
company; but we 're having pretty good times now
among ourselves."

Ruth knew what the "no company" meant; just that
there was no regular inviting, and so no slight in asking
her alone, out of her family; but she knew the Marchbanks parlors were always full of an evening, and that
the usual set would be pretty sure to get together, and
that the end of it all would be an impromptu German, for

which she should play, and that the Marchbanks's man would be sent home with her at eleven o'clock.

She only thanked Adelaide, and said she "did n't know,— perhaps; but she hardly thought she could to-night; they had better not expect her," and got away without promising. She was thinking it over now.

She did not want to be stiff and disobliging; and she would like to hear Mrs. Van Alstyne sing. If it were only for herself, she would very likely think it a reasonable "quid pro quo," and modestly acknowledge that she had no claim to absolutely gratuitous compliment. She would remember higher reason, also, than the *quid pro quo ;* she would try to be glad in this little special "gift of ministering"; but it puzzled her about the others. How would they feel about it ? Would they like it, her being asked so ? Would they think she ought to go ? And what if she were to get into this way of being asked alone ? — she the very youngest; not "in society" yet even as much as Rose and Barbara; though Barbara said *they* "never ' came ' out, — they just leaked out."

That was it; that would not do; she must not leak out, away from them, with her little waltz ripples; if there were any small help or power of hers that could be counted in to make them all more valued, she would not take it from the family fund and let it be counted alone to her sole credit. It must go with theirs. It was little enough that she could repay into the household that had given itself to her like a born home.

She thought she would not even ask Mrs. Holabird anything about it, as at first she meant to do.

But Mrs. Holabird had a way of coming right into

things. "We girls" means Mrs. Holabird as much as
anybody. It was always "we girls" in her heart, since
girls' mothers never can quite lose the girl out of themselves; it only multiplies, and the "everlasting nominative" turns into a plural.

Ruth still sat in her white chair, with her cheek on
her hand and her elbow on the window-ledge, looking
out across the pleasant swell of grass to where they were
cutting the first hay in old Mr. Holabird's five-acre field,
the click of the mowing-machine sounding like some new,
gigantic kind of grasshopper, chirping its tremendous
laziness upon the lazy air, when mother came in from the
front hall, through her own room and saw her there.

Mrs. Holabird never came through the rooms without
a fresh thrill of pleasantness. Her home had *expressed*
itself here, as it had never done anywhere else. There
was something in the fair, open, sunshiny roominess and
cosey connection of these apartments, hers and her
daughters', in harmony with the largeness and cheeriness
and dearness in which her love and her wish for them
held them always.

It was more glad than grand; and she aimed at no
grandness; but the generous space was almost splendid
in its effect, as you looked through, especially to her who
had lived and contrived in a "spy-glass house" so long.

The doors right through from front to back, and the
wide windows at either end and all the way, gave such
sweep and light; also the long mirrors, that had been
from time unrememberable over the mantels in the
town parlors, in the old, useless, horizontal style, and
were here put, quite elegantly tall, — the one in Mrs.

Holabird's **room above** her daintily appointed dressing-table (which **was** only **two** great square **trunks** full of blankets, **that** could not be stowed away anywhere else, dressed up **in** delicate-patterned chintz **and set with** her boxes and cushions **and** toilet-bottles), and the other, **in** " the girls' room," opposite ; these made magnificent reflections and repetitions ; **and** at night, when **they all** lit their bed-candles, and vibrated **back** and forth with their last words before they shut their doors and subsided, gave **a truly** festival and illuminated air **to** the **whole** mansion ; **so** that **Mrs.** Roderick would often ask, when **she came** in of a **morning in** their busiest time, " Did you **have** company last night ? **I** saw you **were** all lit up."

" We had one candle **apiece,"** Barbara would answer, **very** concisely.

"**I do** wish all **our windows** did n't **look** Mrs. Roder-**ick's way,"** Rosamond said once, **after she** had gone.

"**And that** she *did* n't have **to** come through **our** clothes-yard **of a** Monday morning, to see just how many white skirts we have in the wash," added Barbara.

But this **is off the track.**

" **What is it, Ruth ?** " asked **Mrs.** Holabird, **as she came in upon the little figure in** the white chair, midway **in the long** light through the open rooms. " You did n't **really mind** Stephen, did **you ? "**

" O no, indeed, **aunt ! I was** only thinking out things. I believe I 've done, pretty nearly. I guess I sha' n't go. I wanted to make sure I was n't provoked."

" **You 're talking from** where you left off, are n't **you,** Ruthie ? "

" Yes, I guess **so,"** said Ruth, laughing. " It seems

like talking right on, — does n't it ? — when you speak suddenly out of a 'think.' I wonder what *alone* really means. It does n't ever quite seem alone. Something thinks alongside always, or else you could n't keep it up."

"Are you making an essay on metaphysics? You 're a queer little Ruth."

"Am I?" Ruth laughed again. "I can't help it. It *does* answer back."

"And what was the answer about this time?"

That was how Ruth came to let it out.

"About going over to the Marchbanks's to-night. Don't say anything, though. I thought they need n't have asked me just to play. And they might have asked somebody with me. Of course it would have been as you said, if I 'd wanted to ; but I 've made up my mind I — need n't. I mean, I knew right off that I *did n't*."

Ruth did talk a funny idiom of her own when she came out of one of her thinks. But Mrs. Holabird understood. Mothers get to understand the older idiom, just as they do baby-talk, — by the same heart-key. She knew that the " need n't " and the " did n't " referred to the " wanting to."

"You see, I don't think it would be a good plan to let them begin with me so."

"You 're a very sagacious little Ruth," said Mrs. Holabird, affectionately. " And a very generous one."

"No, indeed!" Ruth exclaimed at that. "I believe I think it 's rather nice to settle that I *can* be contrary. I don't like to be pat-a-caked."

She was glad, afterward, that Mrs. Holabird understood.

The next morning Elinor Hadden and Leslie Gold-thwaite walked over, to ask the girls to go down into the wood-hollow to get azaleas.

Rosamond and Ruth went. Barbara was busy: she was more apt to be the busy one of a morning than Rosamond; not because Rosamond was not willing, but that when she *was* at leisure she looked as though she always had been and always expected to be; she would have on a cambric morning-dress, and a jimpsey bit of an apron, and a pair of little fancy slippers, — (there was a secret about Rosamond's slippers; she had half a dozen different ways of getting them up, with braiding, and beading, and scraps of cloth and velvet; and these tops would go on to any stray soles she could get hold of, that were more sole than body, in a way she only knew of;) and she would have the sitting-room at the last point of morning fresh-ness, — chairs and tables and books in the most charming relative positions, and every little leaf and flower in vase or basket just set as if it had so peeped up itself among the others, and all new-born to-day. So it was her gift to be ready and to receive. Barbara, if she really might have been dressed, would be as likely as not to be comfortable in a sack and skirt and her " points," — as she called her black prunella shoes, that were weak at the heels and go-ing at the sides, and kept their original character only by these embellishments upon the instep, — and to have dumped herself down on the broad lower stair in the hall, just behind the green blinds of the front entrance, with a chapter to finish in some irresistible book, or a pair of stockings to mend.

Rosamond was only thankful when she was behind the

scenes and would stay there, not bouncing into the door-
way from the dining-room, with unexpected little bobs, a
cake-bowl in one hand and an egg-beater in the other, to
get what she called "grabs of conversation."

Of course she did not do this when the Marchbankses
were there, or if Miss Pennington called ; but she could
not resist the Haddens and Leslie Goldthwaite ; besides,
" they *did* have to make their own cake, and why should
they be ashamed of it ? "

Rosamond would reply that "they *did* have to make
their own beds, but they could not bring them down stairs
for parlor work."

" That was true, and reason why : they just could n't ;
if they could, she would make up hers all over the house,
just where there was the most fun. She hated pretences,
and being fine."

Rosamond met the girls on the piazza to-day, when she
saw them coming; for Barbara was particularly awful at
this moment, with a skimmer and a very red face, doing
raspberries ; and she made them sit down there in the
shaker chairs, while she ran to get her hat and boots, and
to call Ruth ; and the first thing Barbara saw of them was
from the kitchen window, " slanting off " down over the
croquet-ground toward the big trees.

Somebody overtook and joined them there, — somebody
in a dark gray suit and bright buttons.

" Why, that," cried Barbara, all to herself and her up-
lifted skimmer, looking after them, — " that must be the
brother from West Point the Inglesides expected, — that
young Dakie Thayne ! "

It was Dakie Thayne ; who, after they had all been in-

troduced and were walking on comfortably together, asked
Ruth Holabird if it had not been she who had been expected and wanted so badly last night at Mrs. Marchbanks's ?

Ruth dropped a little back as she walked with him, at
the moment, behind the others, along the path between
the chestnut-trees.

"I don't think they quite expected me. I told Adelaide
I did not think I could come. I am the youngest, you
see," she said with a smile, "and I don't go out very
much, except with my — cousins."

" Your cousins ? I fancied you were all sisters."

"It is all the same," said Ruth. "And that is why I always catch my breath a little before I say ' cousins.'"

"Could n't they come? What a pity!" pursued this young man, who seemed bent upon driving his questions home.

"O, it was n't an invitation, you know. It was n't company."

"Was n't it?"

The inflection was almost imperceptible, and quite unintentional; Dakie Thayne was very polite; but his eyebrows went up a little — just a line or two — as he said it, the light beginning to come in upon him.

Dakie had been about in the world somewhat; his two years at West Point were not all his experience; and he knew what queer little wheels were turned sometimes.

He had just come to Z—— (I must have a letter for my nameless town, and I have gone through the whole alphabet for it, and picked up a crooked stick at last), and the new group of people he had got among interested him. He liked problems and experiments. They were what he excelled in at the Military School. This was his first furlough; and it was since his entrance at the Academy that his brother, Dr. Ingleside, had come to Z——, to take the vacant practice of an old physician, disabled from continuing it.

Dakie and Leslie Goldthwaite and Mrs. Ingleside were old friends; almost as old as Mrs. Ingleside and the doctor.

Ruth Holabird had a very young girl's romance of admiration for one older, in her feeling toward Leslie. She had never known any one just like her; and, in truth,

Leslie was different, **in** some things, from **the** little world **of** girls about her.   **In the** " each and all " of their pretty groupings and pleasant relations she was like a bit of fresh, springing, delicate vine in a bouquet of bright, similarly beautiful flowers ; taking little free curves **and** reaches of her own, just as she had grown ; not tied, nor **placed, nor** constrained ; **never the** central or most brilliant thing **; but** somehow **a kind of life** and grace that helped and touched and perfected **all.**

There was something **very** real and individual about her ; she **was** no **" girl** of the period," made **up** by the **fashion of the** day.   She would have grown just as a rose **or a violet** would, the **same in** the first **quarter of** the cen- **tury or the third.   They** called her " grandmotherly " sometimes, **when a** certain quaint primitiveness that was **in her** showed itself.   **And yet** she was the youngest girl **in** all that set, as to simpleness and freshness and unpre- tendingness, though she **was** in her twentieth year now, which sounds — did n't somebody say so over my shoul- der ? — so very old ! Adelaide Marchbanks used **to say of** her that **she** had " stayed fifteen."

She *looked* **real.   Her** bright hair was gathered up **loosely, with** some graceful turn that showed its fine shin- **ing** strands **had all** been freshly dressed and handled, un- der **a** wide-meshed net that **lay** lightly around her head ; **it was** not packed and stuffed and matted and put on like **a** pad **or** bolster, from the bump of benevolence, all over that and everything else gentle and beautiful, down to the bend of her neck ; and her dress suggested always some one simple idea which you could trace through it, in **its** harmony, at a glance ; **not complex and** bewildering and fatiguing with its many parts and folds and festoonings and the garnishings of every one of these. She looked more as young women used to look before it took a lady with her dressmaker seven toilsome days to achieve a "short street suit," and the public promenades became the problems that they now are to the inquiring minds that are forced to wonder who stops at home and does up all the sewing, and where the hair all comes from.

Some of the girls said, sometimes, that "Leslie Gold-thwaite liked to be odd; she took pains to be." This was not true; she began with the prevailing fashion — the fundamental idea of it — always, when she had a new thing; but she modified and curtailed, — something was sure to stop her somewhere; and the trouble with the new fashions is that they never stop. To use a phrase she had picked up a few years ago, "something always got crowded out." She had other work to do, and she must choose the finishing that would take the shortest time; or satin folds would cost six dollars more, and she wanted the money to use differently; the dress was never the first and the *must be;* so it came by natural develop-ment to express herself, not the rampant mode; and her little ways of "dodging the dressmaker," as she called it, were sure to be graceful, as well as adroit and decided.

It was a good thing for a girl like Ruth, just growing up to questions that had first come to this other girl of nineteen four years ago, that this other had so met them one by one, and decided them half unconsciously as she went along, that now, for the great puzzle of the "out-side," which is getting more and more between us and our real living, there was this one more visible, unobtru-

sive answer put ready, and with such a charm of attrac-
tiveness, into the world.

Ruth walked behind her this morning, with Dakie
Thayne, thinking how " achy " Elinor Hadden's puffs and
French-blue bands, and bits of embroidery looked, for
the stitches somebody had put into them, and the weary
starching and ironing and perking out that must be done
for them, beside the simple hem and the one narrow
basque ruffling of Leslie's cambric morning-dress, which
had its color and its set-off in itself, in the bright little
carnations with brown stems that figured it. It was
" trimmed in the piece "; and that was precisely what
Leslie had said when she chose it. She "dodged" a
great deal in the mere buying.

Leslie and Ruth got together in the wood-hollow,
where the little vines and ferns began. Leslie was quick
to spy the bits of creeping Mitchella, and the wee feathery
fronds that hid away their miniature grace under the feet
of their taller sisters. They were so pretty to put in
shells, and little straight tube-vases. Dakie Thayne
helped Rose and Elinor to get the branches of white
honeysuckle that grew higher up.

Rose walked with the young cadet, the arms of both
filled with the fragrant-flowering stems, as they came up
homeward again. She was full of bright, pleasant chat.
It just suited her to spend a morning so, as if there were
no rooms to dust and no tables to set, in all the great
sunshiny world; but as if dews freshened everything, and
furnishings " came," and she herself were clothed of the
dawn and the breeze, like a flower. She never cared so
much for afternoons, she said; of course one had got

through with the prose by that time; but "to go off like a bird or a bee right after breakfast, — that was living; that was the Irishman's blessing, — 'the top o' the mornin' till yez!'"

"Won't you come in and have some lunch?" she asked, with the most magnificent intrepidity, when she had n't the least idea what there would be to give them all if they did, as they came round under the piazza basement, and up to the front portico.

They thanked her, no; they must get home with their flowers; and Mrs. Ingleside expected Dakie to an early dinner.

Upon which she bade them good by, standing among her great azalea branches, and looking "awfully pretty," as Dakie Thayne said afterward, precisely as if she had nothing else to think of.

The instant they had fairly moved away, she turned and ran in, in a hurry to look after the salt-cellars, and to see that Katty had n't got the table-cloth diagonal to the square of the room instead of parallel, or committed any of the other general-housework horrors which she detailed herself on daily duty to prevent.

Barbara stood behind the blind.

"The audacity of that!" she cried, as Rosamond came in. "I shook right out of my points when I heard you! Old Mrs. Lovett has been here, and has eaten up exactly the last slice of cake but one. So that's Dakie Thayne?"

"Yes. He's a nice little fellow. Are n't these lovely flowers?"

"O my gracious! that great six-foot cadet!"

"It does n't matter about the feet. He's barely eigh'een. But he's nice, — ever so nice."

" **It 's a** case **of** Outledge, Leslie," Dakie Thayne said, going down the **hill.** " They treat those girls — amphibiously ! "

" **Well,**" returned Leslie, laughing, " *I 'm* amphibious. I live in the town, and I *can* come out — and not die — on the Hill. I like **it.** I always thought that kind of animal had the nicest time."

They met Alice Marchbanks with her cousin Maud, coming up.

" We 've **been to see the** Holabirds," said Dakie Thayne, right off.

" I wonder why that little Ruth **did n't come** last night ? **We really** wanted her," said Alice to Leslie Goldthwaite.

" **For** batrachian reasons, **I** believe," put in Dakie, full of fun. " **She is n't** quite amphibious **yet.** She don't **come** out from **under water.** That **is, she 's** young, and does n't go alone. She told me **so.**"

You need n't keep asking how we know! Things that belong get together. People who tell **a story see** round corners.

The next morning **Maud** Marchbanks came over, and asked us all to play croquet and drink tea with them that **evening,** with **the** Goldthwaites and the Haddens.

" **We 're** growing **very** gay **and** multitudinous," **she said,** graciously.

" The midshipman 's got home, — Harry Goldthwaite, **you** know."

Ruth **was** glad, then, that mother knew ; she had the girls' pride **in her** own keeping ; there was no responsibility of telling **or** withholding. **But** she was glad **also that she had not gone** last night.

When we went up stairs at bedtime, Rosamond asked Barbara the old, inevitable question, —

"What have you got to wear, Barb, to-morrow night, — that's ready?"

And Barbara gave, in substance, the usual unperturbed answer, "Not a dud!"

But Mrs. Holabird kept a garnet and white striped silk skirt on purpose to lend to Barbara. If she had *given* it, there would have been the end. And among us there would generally be a muslin waist, and perhaps an over-skirt. Barbara said our "overskirts" were skirts that were *over with*, before the new fashion came.

Barbara went to bed like a chicken, sure that in the big world to-morrow there would be something that she could pick up.

It was a miserable plan, perhaps; but it *was* one of our ways at Westover.

CHAPTER III.

BETWIXT AND BETWEEN.

THREE things came of the March-banks's party for us Holabirds.

Mrs. Van Alstyne took a great fancy to Rosamond.

Harry Goldthwaite put a new idea into Barbara's head.

And Ruth's little undeveloped plans, which the facile fingers were to carry out, received a fresh and sudden impetus.

You have thus the three heads of the present chapter.

How could any one help taking a fancy to Rosamond Hola-bird? In the first place, as Mrs. Van Alstyne said, there was the name, — " a making for anybody "; for names do go a great way, notwithstanding Shakespeare.

It made you think of everything springing and singing and blooming and sweet. Its expression was " blossomy, nightingale-y "; atilt with glee and grace. And that was the way she looked and seemed. If you spoke to her

suddenly, the head turned as a bird's does, with a small,
shy, all-alive movement; and the bright eye glanced up
at you, ready to catch electric meanings from your own.
When she talked to you in return, she talked all over;
with quiet, refined radiations of life and pleasure in each
involuntary turn and gesture; the blossom of her face
lifted and swayed like that of a flower delicately poised
upon its stalk. She was *like* a flower chatting with a
breeze.

She forgot altogether, as a present fact, that she looked
pretty; but she had known it once, when she dressed herself, and been glad of it; and something lasted from the
gladness just enough to keep out of her head any painful,
conscious question of how she *was* seeming. That, and
her innate sense of things proper and refined, made her
manners what Mrs. Van Alstyne pronounced them, —
"exquisite."

That was all Mrs. Van Alstyne waited to find out.
She did not go deep; hence she took quick fancies or dis-
likes, and a great many of them.

She got Rosamond over into a corner with herself, and
they had everybody round them. All the people in the
room were saying how lovely Miss Holabird looked to-
night. For a little while that seemed a great and beautiful
thing. I don't know whether it was or not. It was
pleasant to have them find it out; but she would have
been just as lovely if they had not. Is a party so very
particular a thing to be lovely in? I wonder what makes
the difference. She might have stood on that same square
of the Turkey carpet the next day and been just as pretty.
But, somehow, it seemed grand in the eyes of us girls,

and it meant a great deal that it would not mean the next day, to have her stand right there, and look just so, to-night.

In the midst of it all, though, Ruth saw something that seemed to her grander, — another girl, in another corner, looking on, — a girl with a very homely face ; somebody's cousin, brought with them there. She looked pleased and self-forgetful, differently from Rose in her prettiness ; *she* looked as if she had put herself away, comfortably satis-fied ; this one looked as if there were no self put away anywhere. Ruth turned round to Leslie Goldthwaite, who stood by.

"I do think," she said, — "don't you? — it's just the bravest and strongest thing in the world to be awfully homely, and to know it, and to go right on and have a good time just the same ; — *every day*, you see, right through everything ! I think such people must be splen-did inside ! "

" The most splendid person I almost ever knew was like that," said Leslie. " And she was fifty years old too."

" Well," said Ruth, drawing a girl's long breath at the fifty years, "it was pretty much over then, was n't it ? But I think I should like — just once — to look beautiful at a party ! "

The best of it for Barbara had been on the lawn, before tea.

Barbara was a magnificent croquet-player. She and Harry Goldthwaite were on one side, and they led off their whole party, going nonchalantly through wicket after wicket, as if they could not help it ; and after they had

well distanced the rest, just toling each other along over
the ground, till they were rovers together, and came down
into the general field again with havoc to the enemy, and
the whole game in their hands on their own part.

"It was a handsome thing to see, for once," Dakie
Thayne said; "but they might make much of it, for it
would n't do to let them play on the same side again."

It was while they were off, apart down the slope, just
croqueted away for the time, to come up again with tremendous charge presently, that Harry asked her if she
knew the game of " ship-coil."

Barbara shook her head.   What was it?

" It is a pretty thing.   The officers of a Russian frigate showed it to us.   They play it with rings made of spliced rope ; we had them plain enough, but you might make them as gay as you liked.   There are ten rings, and each player throws them all at each turn.   The object is to string them up over a stake, from which you stand at a certain distance.   Whatever number you make counts up for your side, and you play as many rounds as you may agree upon."

Barbara thought a minute, and then looked up quickly.

" Have you told anybody else of that ? "

" Not here.   I have n't thought of it for a good while."

" Would you just please, then," said Barbara in a hurry, as somebody came down toward them in pursuit of a ball, " to hush up, and let me have it all to myself for a while ?   And then," she added, as the stray ball was driven up the lawn again, and the player went away after it, " come some day and help us get it up at Westover? It 's such a thing, you see, to get anything that 's new."

" I see.   To be sure.   You shall have the State Right, — is n't that what they make over for patent concerns ?   And we 'll have something famous out of it. They 're getting tired of croquet, or thinking they ought to be, which is the same thing."   It was Barbara's turn now ; she hit Harry Goldthwaite's ball with one of her precise little taps, and, putting the two beside each other with her mallet, sent them up rollicking into the thick of the fight, where the final hand-to-hand struggle was taking place between the last two wickets and the stake.   Everybody was there in a bunch when she came ; in a minute everybody of the opposing party was everywhere else, and she and Harry had it between them again. She played out two balls, and then, accidentally, her own. After one " distant, random gun," from the discomfited foe, Harry rolled quietly up against the wand, and the game was over.

It was then and there that a frank, hearty liking and alliance was re-established between Harry Goldthwaite and Barbara, upon an old remembered basis of ten years ago, when he had gone away to school and given her half his marbles for a parting keepsake, — " as he might have done," we told her, " to any other boy."

" Ruth has n't had a good time," said mother, softly, standing in her door, looking through at the girls laying away ribbons and pulling down hair, and chattering as only girls in their teens do chatter at bedtime.

Ruth was in her white window-chair, one foot up on a cricket ; and, as if she could not get into that place without her considering-fit coming over her, she sat with her one unlaced boot in her hand, and her eyes away out over the moonlighted fields.

" She played all the evening, nearly. She always does," said Barbara.

" Why, I had a splendid time ! " cried Ruth, coming down upon them out of her cloud with flat contradiction. " And I 'm sure I did n't play all the evening. Mrs. Van Alstyne sang Tennyson's ' Brook,' aunt ; and the music *splashes* so in it ! It did really seem as if she were spattering it all over the room, and it was n't a bit of matter ! "

" The time was *so* good, then, that it has made you sober," said Mrs. Holabird, coming and putting her hand on

4

the back of the white chair. " I 've known good times **do that.**"

" It has given me ever so much thinking **to do ;** besides that brook **in** my head, ' going on forever — ever ! *go*-ing-on-forever ! ' " And Ruth broke into the **joyous** refrain **of the** song as she ended.

" I shall come **to** you for a great long talk **to-morrow** morning, mother ! " Ruth said again, turning **her head** and touching her lips **to** the mother-hand on her chair. She **did not** always say "mother," **you** see ; **it was only** when she wanted **a very dear word.**

" We 'll wind the rings with all the pretty-colored stuffs **we can find in** the bottomless piece-bag," Barbara was **saying, at** the same moment, in the **room** beyond. " And **you can bring out your old** ribbon-box for the bowing-up, Rosamond. **It's a charity to** clear out **your** glory-holes once in **a while.** It 's going to be just — splend-umphant ! "

" If you don 't go and talk about it," said Rosamond. " We *must* keep the new **of** it to ourselves."

" As if I needed ! " cried Barbara, indignantly. " When **I hushed up Harry** Goldthwaite, and went round **all** the rest of the evening **without** doing anything **but** just give **you that awful** little **pinch ! "**

" That was bad enough," said Rosamond, quietly ; she **never got cross or** inelegantly excited about anything. " But **I** *do* think the girls will like **it.** And **we** might **have tea out on** the broad piazza."

" That is bare **floor too,**" said Barbara, mischievously.

Now, our dining-room had not yet even the English drugget. The dark **new** boards would do for **summer** weather, mother said. " If it had been real oak, polished ! " Rosamond thought. " But hard-pine was kitcheny."

Ruth went to bed with the rest of her thinking and the brook-music flittering in her brain.

Mrs. Lewis Marchbanks had talked behind her with Jeannie Hadden about her playing. It was not the compliment that excited her so, although they said her touch and expression were wonderful, and that her fingers were like little flying magnets, that could n't miss the right points. Jeannie Hadden said she liked to *see* Ruth Holabird play, as well as she did to hear her.

But it was Mrs. Marchbanks's saying that she would give almost anything to have Lily taught such a style; she hardly knew what she should do with her; there was no good teacher in the town who gave lessons at the houses, and Lily was not strong enough to go regularly to Mr. Viertelnote. Besides, she had picked up a story of his being cross, and rapping somebody's fingers, and Lily was very shy and sensitive. She never did herself any justice if she began to be afraid.

Jeannie Hadden said it was just her mother's trouble about Reba, except that Reba was strong enough; only that Mrs. Hadden preferred a teacher to come to the house.

"A good young-lady teacher, to give beginners a desirable style from the very first, is exceedingly needed since Miss Robbyns went away," said Mrs. Marchbanks, to whom just then her sister came and said something, and drew her off.

Ruth's fingers flew over the keys; and it must have been magnetism that guided them, for in her brain quite other quick notes were struck, and ringing out a busy chime of their own.

"If I only could!" she was saying to herself. "If they really would have me, and they would let me at home. Then I could go to Mr. Viertelnote. I think I could do it! I'm almost sure! I could show anybody what I know, — and if they like that!"

It went over and over now, as she lay wakeful in bed, mixed up with the "forever — ever," and the dropping tinkle of that lovely trembling ripple of accompaniment, until the late moon got round to the south and slanted in between the white dimity curtains, and set a glimmering little ghost in the arm-chair.

Ruth came down late to breakfast.

Barbara was pushing back her chair.

"Mother, — or anybody! Do you want any errand down in town? I'm going out for a stramble. A party always has to be walked off next morning."

"And talked off, does n't it? I'm afraid my errand would need to be with Mrs. Goldthwaite or Mrs. Hadden, would n't it?"

"Well, I dare say I shall go in and see Leslie. Rosamond, why can't you come too? It's a sort of nuisance that boy having come home!"

"That 'great six-foot lieutenant'!" parodied Rose.

"I don't care! You said feet did n't signify. And he used to be a boy, when we played with him so."

"I suppose they all used to be," said Rose, demurely.

"Well, I won't go! Because the truth is I did want to see him, about those — patent rights. I dare say they 'll come up."

"I 've no doubt," said Rosamond.

"I wish you *would* both go away somewhere," said

Ruth, as Mrs. Holabird gave her her coffee. "Because I and mother have got a secret, and I know she wants her last little hot corner of toast."

"I think you are likely to get the last little cold corner," said Mrs. Holabird, as Ruth sat, forgetting her plate, after the other girls had gone away.

"I'm thinking, mother, of a real warm little corner! Something that would just fit in and make everything so nice. It was put into my head last night, and I think it was sent on purpose; it came right up behind me so. Mrs. Lewis Marchbanks and Jeannie Hadden praised my playing; more than I could tell you, really; and Mrs. Marchbanks wants a —" Ruth stopped, and laughed at the word that was coming — "*lady*-teacher for Lily, and so does Mrs. Hadden for Reba. There, mother. It's in *your* head now! Please turn it over with a nice little think, and tell me you would just as lief, and that you believe perhaps I could!"

By this time Ruth was round behind Mrs. Holabird's chair, with her two hands laid against her cheeks. Mrs. Holabird leaned her face down upon one of the hands, holding it so, caressingly.

"I am sure you could, Ruthie. But I am sure I *would n't* just as lief! I would liefer you should have all you need without."

"I know that, mother. But it would n't be half so good for me!"

"That's something horrid, I know!" exclaimed Barbara, coming in upon the last word. "It always is, when people talk about its being good for them. It's sure to be salts or senna, and most likely both."

"O dear me!" said Ruth, suddenly seized with a new perception of difficulty. Until now, she had only been considering whether she could, and if Mrs. Holabird would approve. "*Don't* you — or Rose — call it names, Barbara, please, will you?"

"Which of us are you most afraid of? For Rosamond's salts and senna are different from mine, pretty often. I guess it's hers this time, by your putting her in that anxious parenthesis."

"I'm afraid of your fun, Barbara, and I'm afraid of Rosamond's — "

"Earnest? Well, that is much the more frightful. It is so awfully quiet and pretty-behaved and positive. But if you're going to retain me on your side, you'll have to lay the case before me, you know, and give me a fee. You needn't stand there, bribing the judge beforehand."

Ruth turned right round and kissed Barbara.

"I want you to go with me and see if Mrs. Hadden and Mrs. Lewis Marchbanks would let me teach the children."

"Teach the children! What?"

"O, music, of course. That's all I know, pretty much. And — make Rose understand."

"Ruth, you're a duck! I like you for it! But I'm not sure I like *it*."

"Will you do just those two things?"

"It's a beautiful programme. But suppose we leave out the first part? I think you could do that alone. It would spoil it if I went. It's such a nice little spontaneous idea of your own, you see. But if we made it a regular family delegation — besides, it will take as much as

all me to manage the second. Rosamond is very elegant to-day. Last night's twilight is n't over. And it 's
funny *we* 've plans too ; *we* 're going to give lessons, —
differently ; we 're going to lead off, for once, — we Holabirds ; and I don't know exactly how the music will
chime in. It *may* make things — Holabirdy."

Rosamond had true perceptions, and she was consci-
entious. What she said, therefore, when she was told,
was, —

" O dear ! I suppose it is right ! But — just now !
Right things do come in so terribly askew, like good old
Mr. Isosceles, sidling up the broad aisle of a Sunday !
Could n't you wait awhile, Ruth ? "

" And then somebody else would get the chance."

" There 's nobody else to be had."

" Nobody knows till somebody starts up. They don't
know there 's *me* to be had yet."

" O Ruth ! Don't offer to teach grammar, anyhow !"

" I don't know. I might. I should n't *teach* it ' anyhow.' "

Ruth went off, laughing, happy. She knew she had
gamed the home-half of her point.

Her heart beat a good deal, though, when she went into
Mrs. Marchbanks's library alone, and sat waiting for the
lady to come down.

She would rather have gone to Mrs. Hadden first, who
was very kind and old-fashioned, and not so overpower-
ingly grand. But she had her justification for her attempt
from Mrs. Marchbanks's own lips, and she must take up
her opportunity as it came to her, following her clew right
end first. She meant simply to tell Mrs. Marchbanks how
she had happened to think of it.

"Good morning," said the great lady, graciously, wondering not a little what had brought the child, in this un-
ceremonious early fashion, to ask for her.

"I came," said Ruth, after she had answered the good
morning, "because I heard what you were so kind as to
say last night about liking my playing; and that you had
nobody just now to teach Lily. I thought, perhaps, you
might be willing to try me; for I should like to do it, and
I think I could show her all I know; and then I could
take lessons myself of Mr. Viertelnote. I've been thinking about it all night."

Ruth Holabird had a direct little fashion of going
straight through whatever crust of outside appearance to
that which must respond to what she had at the moment
in herself. She had real *self-possession;* because she did
not let herself be magnetized into a false consciousness of
somebody else's self, and think and speak according to
their notions of things, or her reflected notion of what
they would think of her. She was different from Rosamond in this; Rosamond could not help *feeling her
double,*— Mrs. Grundy's "idea" of her. That was what
Rosamond said herself about it, when Ruth told it all at
home.

The response is almost always there to those who go for
it; if it is not, there is no use any way.

Mrs. Marchbanks smiled.

"Does Mrs. Holabird know?"

"O yes; she always knows."

There was a little distance and a touch of business in
Mrs. Marchbanks's manner after this. The child's own
impulse had been very frank and amusing; an authorized

seeking of employment was somewhat different. Still, she was kind enough; the impression had been made; perhaps Rosamond, with her "just now" feeling, would have been sensitive to what did not touch Ruth, at the moment, at all.

"But you see, my dear, that *your* having a pupil could not be quite equal to Mr. Viertelnote's doing the same thing. I mean the one would not quite provide for the other."

"O no, indeed! I'm in hopes to have two. I mean to go and see Mrs. Hadden about Reba; and then I might begin first, you know. If I could teach two quarters, I could take one."

"You have thought it all over. You are quite a little business woman. Now let us see. I do like your playing, Ruth. I think you have really a charming style. But whether you could *impart* it,—that is a different capacity."

"I am pretty good at showing how," said Ruth. "I think I could make her understand all I do."

"Well; I should be willing to pay twenty dollars a quarter to any lady who would bring Lily forward to where you are; if you can do it, I will pay it to you. If Mrs. Hadden will do the same, you will have two thirds of Viertelnote's price."

"O, that is so nice!" said Ruth, gratefully. "Then in half a quarter I could begin. And perhaps in that time I might get another."

"I shall be exceedingly interested in your getting on," said Mrs. Marchbanks, as Ruth arose to go. She said it very much as she might have said it to anybody

who was going to try to earn money, and whom she
meant to patronize. But Ruth took it singly; she was
not two persons, — one who asked for work and pay, and
another who expected to be treated as if she were privi-
leged above either. She was quite intent upon her purpose.

If Mrs. Marchbanks had been patron kind, Mrs. Hadden was motherly so.

"You 're a dear little thing ! When will you begin ?"
said she.

Ruth's morning was a grand success. She came home
with a rapid step, springing to a soundless rhythm.

She found Rosamond and Barbara and Harry Goldthwaite on the piazza, winding the rope rings with blue
and scarlet and white and purple, and tying them with
knots of ribbon.

Harry had been prompt enough. He had got the rope,
and spliced it up himself, that morning, and had brought
the ten rings over, hanging upon his arms like bangles.

They were still busy when dinner was ready; and Harry
stayed at the first asking.

It was a scrub-day in the kitchen ; and Katty came in
to take the plates with her sleeves rolled up, a smooch of
stove-polish across her arm, and a very indiscriminate-
colored apron. She put one plate upon another in a hurry, over knives and forks and remnants, clattered a good
deal, and dropped the salt-spoons.

Rosamond colored and frowned ; but talked with a most
resolutely beautiful repose.

Afterward, when it was all over, and Harry had gone,
promising to come next day and bring a stake, painted

vermilion and white, with a little gilt ball on the top of it, she sat by the ivied window in the brown room with tears in her eyes.

" It is dreadful to live so ! " she said, with real feeling. " To have just one wretched girl to do everything ! "

" Especially," said Barbara, without much mercy, " when she always *will* do it at dinner-time."

" It's the betwixt and between that I can't bear," said Rose. " To have to do with people like the Penningtons and the Marchbankses, and to see their ways ; to sit at tables where there is noiseless and perfect serving, and to know that they think it is the ' mainspring of life ' (that's just what Mrs. Van Alstyne said about it the other day) ; and then to have to hitch on so ourselves, knowing just as well what ought to be as she does, — it's too bad. It's double dealing. I'd rather not know, or pretend any better. I do wish we *belonged* somewhere ! "

Ruth felt sorry. She always did when Rosamond was hurt with these things. She knew it came from a very pure, nice sense of what was beautiful, and a thoroughness of desire for it. She knew she wanted it *every day*, and that nobody hated shams, or company contrivances, more heartily. She took great trouble for it ; so that when they were quite alone, and Rosamond could manage, things often went better than when guests came and divided her attention.

Ruth went over to where she sat.

" Rose, perhaps we *do* belong just here. Somebody has got to be in the shading-off, you know. That helps both ways."

" It's a miserable indefiniteness, though."

"No, it is n't," said Barbara, quickly. "It's a good plan, and I like it. Ruth just hits it. I see now what they mean by 'drawing lines.' You can't draw them anywhere but in the middle of the stripes. And people that are *right* in the middle have to 'toe the mark.' It's the edge, after all. You can reach a great deal farther by being betwixt and between. And one girl need n't *always* be black-leaded, nor drop all the spoons."

CHAPTER IV.

NEXT THINGS.

ROSAMOND'S ship-coil party was a great success. It resolved itself into Rosamond's party, although Barbara had had the first thought of it; for Rosamond quietly took the management of all that was to be delicately and gracefully arranged, and to have the true tone of high propriety.

Barbara made the little white rolls; Rosamond and Ruth beat up the cake; mother attended to the boiling of the tongues, and, when it was time, to the making of the delicious coffee; all together we gave all sorts of pleasant touches to the brown room, and set the round table (the old cover could be " shied " out of sight now, as Stephen said, and replaced with the white glistening damask for the tea) in the corner between the southwest windows that opened upon the broad piazza.

The table was bright with pretty silver — not too much

—and best glass and delicate porcelain with a tiny thread
of gold; and the rolls and the thin strips of tongue cut
lengthwise, so rich and tender that a fork could manage
them, and the large raspberries, black and red and white,
were upon plates and dishes of real Indian, white and
golden brown.

The wide sashes were thrown up, and there were light
chairs outside; Mrs. Holabird would give the guests tea
and coffee, and Ruth and Barbara would sit in the window-
seats and do the waiting, back and forth, and Dakie
Thayne and Harry Goldthwaite would help.

Katty held her office as a sinecure that day; looked on
admiringly, forgot half her regular work, felt as if she had
somehow done wonders without realizing the process, and
pronounced that it was " no throuble at ahl to have company."

But before the tea was the new game.

It was a bold stroke for us Holabirds. Originating was
usually done higher up; as the Papal Council gives forth
new spiritual inventions for the joyful acceptance of be-
lievers, who may by no means invent in their turn and
offer to the Council. One could hardly tell how it would
fall out, — whether the Haddens and the Marchbankses
would take to it, or whether it would drop right there.

"They *may* 'take it off your hands, my dear,'" suggested the remorseless Barbara. Somebody had offered
to do that once for Mrs. Holabird, when her husband had
had an interest in a ship in the Baltic trade, and some furs
had come home, richer than we had quite expected.

Rose was loftily silent; she would not have *said* that to
her very self; but she had her little quiet instincts of

holding on, — through Harry Goldthwaite, chiefly ; it was his novelty.

Does this seem *very* bare worldly scheming among young girls who should simply have been having a good time ? We should not tell you if we did not know ; it *begins* right there among them, in just such things as these ; and our day and our life are full of it.

The Marchbanks set had a way of taking things off people's hands, as soon as they were proved worth while. People like the Holabirds could not be taking this pains every day ; making their cakes and their coffee, and setting their tea-table in their parlor ; putting aside all that was shabby or inadequate, for a few special hours, and turning all the family resources upon a point, to serve an occasion. But if anything new or bright were so produced that could be transplanted, it was so easy to receive it among the established and every-day elegances of a freer living, give it a wider introduction, and so adopt and repeat and centralize it that the originators should fairly forget they had ever begun it. And why would not this be honor enough ? Invention must always pass over to the capital that can handle it.

The new game charmed them all. The girls had the best of it, for the young men always gathered up the rings and brought them to each in turn. It was very pretty to receive both hands full of the gayly wreathed and knotted hoops, to hold them slidden along one arm like garlands, to pass them lightly from hand to hand again, and to toss them one by one through the air with a motion of more or less inevitable grace ; and the excitement of hope or of success grew with each succeeding trial.

They could not help liking it, even the most fastidious; they might venture upon liking it, for it was a game with an origin and references. It was an officers' game, on board great naval ships; it had proper and sufficient antecedents. It would do.

By the time they stopped playing in the twilight, and went up the wide end steps upon the deep, open platform, where coffee and biscuits began to be fragrant, Rosamond knew that her party was as nice as if it had been anybody's else whoever; that they were all having as genuinely good a time as if they had not come " westover " to get it.

And everybody does like a delicious tea, such as is far more sure and very different from hands like Mrs. Holabird's and her daughters, than from those of a city confectioner and the most professed of private cooks.

It all went off and ended in a glory, — the glory of the sun pouring great backward floods of light and color all up to the summer zenith, and of the softly falling and changing shade, and the slow forth-coming of the stars: and Ruth gave them music, and by and by they had a little German, out there on the long, wide esplanade. It was the one magnificence of their house, — this high, spacious terrace; Rosamond was thankful every day that Grandfather Holabird *had* to build the wood-house under it.

After this, Westover began to grow to be more of a centre than our home, cheery and full of girl-life as it was, had ever been able to become before.

They might have transplanted the game, —they did take slips from it, —and we might not always have had tickets to our own play; but they could not transplant Harry Goldthwaite and Dakie Thayne. They *would* come over, nearly every day, at morning or evening, and practise "coil," or make some other plan or errand; and so there came to be always something going on at the Holabirds', and if the other girls wanted it, they had to come where it was.

Mrs. Van Alstyne came often; Rosamond grew very intimate with her.

Mrs. Lewis Marchbanks did say, one day, that she thought "the Holabirds were slightly mistaking their position"; but the remark did not come round, westover, till long afterward, and meanwhile the position remained the same.

It was right in the midst of all this that Ruth astonished the family again, one evening.

"I wish," she said, suddenly, just as if she were not suggesting something utterly incongruous and disastrous, "that we could ask Lucilla Waters up here for a little visit."

The girls had a way, in Z—, of spending two or three days together at each other's houses, neighbors though they were, within easy reach, and seeing each other almost constantly. Leslie Goldthwaite came up to the Haddens', or they went down to the Goldthwaites'. The Haddens would stay over night at the Marchbanks', and on through the next day, and over night again. There were, indeed, three recognized degrees of intimacy: that which took tea, — that which came in of a morning and stayed to lunch, — and that which was kept over night without plan or ceremony. It had never been very easy for us Holabirds to do such things without plan; of all things, nearly, in the world, it seemed to us sometimes beautiful and desirable to be able to live just so as that we might.

"I wish," said Ruth, "that we could have Lucilla Waters here."

"My gracious!" cried Rosamond, startled into a soft explosion. "What for?"

"Why, I think she'd like it," answered Ruth.

"Well, I suppose Arctura Fish might 'like it' too," responded Rose, in a deadly quiet way now, that was the extreme of sarcasm.

Ruth looked puzzled; as if she really considered what Rosamond suggested, not having thought of it before, and not quite knowing how to dispose of the thought since she had got it.

Dakie Thayne was there; he sat holding some gold-colored wool for Mrs. Holabird to wind; she was giving herself the luxury of some pretty knitting, — making a bright little sofa affghan. Ruth had forgotten him at the instant, speaking out of a quiet pause and her own intent thought.

She made up her mind presently, — partly at least, — and spoke again. "I don't believe," she said, "that it would be the next thing for Arctura Fish."

Dakie Thayne's eyebrows went up, just that half perceptible line or two. "Do you think people ought always to have the next thing?" he asked.

"It seems to me it must be somebody's fault if they don't," replied Ruth.

"It is a long waiting sometimes to get the next thing,"

said Dakie Thayne. "Army men find that out. They grow gray getting it."

."That's where only one *can* have it at a time," said Ruth. "These things are different."

"'Next things' interfere occasionally," said Barbara. "Next things up, and next things down."

"I don't know," said Rose, serenely unconscious and impersonal. "I suppose people would n't naturally — it can't be meant they should — walk right away from their own opportunities."

Ruth laughed, — not aloud, only a little single breath, over her work.

Dakie Thayne leaned back.

"What, — if you please, — Miss Ruth?"

"I was thinking of the opportunities *down*," Ruth answered.

It was several days after this that the young party drifted together again, on the Westover lawn. A plan was discussed. Mrs. Van Alstyne had walked over with Olivia and Adelaide Marchbanks, and it was she who suggested it.

"Why don't you have regular practisings," said she, "and then a meeting, for this and the archery you wanted to get up, and games for a prize? They would do nicely together."

Olivia Marchbanks drew up a little. She had not meant to launch the project here. Everything need not begin at Westover all at once.

But Dakie Thayne broke in.

"Did you think of that?" said he. "It's a capital idea."

"Ideas are rather apt to be that," said Adelaide March-banks. "It is the carrying out, you see."

"Is n't it pretty nearly carried out already? It is only to organize what we are doing as it is."

"But the minute you *do* organize! You don't know how difficult it is in a place like this. A dozen of us are not enough, and as soon as you go beyond, there gets to be too much of it. One does n't know where to stop."

"Or to skip?" asked Harry Goldthwaite, in such a purely bright, good-natured way that no one could take it amiss.

"Well, yes, to skip," said Adelaide. "Of course that's it. You don't go straight on, you know, house by house, when you ask people, — down the hill and into the town."

"We talked it over," said Olivia. "And we got as far as the Hobarts." There Olivia stopped. That was where they had stopped before.

"O yes, the Hobarts; they would be sure to like it," said Leslie Goldthwaite, quick and pleased.

"Her ups and downs are just like yours," said Dakie Thayne to Ruth Holabird.

It made Ruth very glad to be told she was at all like Leslie; it gave her an especially quick pulse of pleasure to have Dakie Thayne say so. She knew he thought there was hardly any one like Leslie Goldthwaite.

"O, they *won't* exactly do, you know!" said Adelaide Marchbanks, with an air of high free-masonry.

"Won't do what?" asked Cadet Thayne, obtusely.

"Suit," replied Olivia, concisely, looking straight forward without any air at all.

"Really, we have tried it since they came," said Ade-

laide; "though what people *come* for is the question, I
think, when there is n't anything particular to bring them
except the neighborhood, and then it has to be Christian
charity in the neighborhood that did n't ask them to pick
them up. Mamma called, after a while; and Mrs. Hobart
said she hoped she would come often, and let *the girls* run
in and be sociable! And Grace Hobart says '*she* has n't
got tired of croquet, — she likes it real well!' They 're
that sort of people, Mr. Thayne."

"Oh! that 's very bad," said Dakie Thayne, with grave
conclusiveness.

"The Haddens had them one night, when we were
going to play commerce. When we asked them up to
the table, they held right back, awfully stiff, and could n't
find anything else to say than, — out quite loud, across
everything, — 'O no! they could n't play commerce;
they never did; father thought it was just like any gam-
bling game!'"

"Plucky, anyhow," said Harry Goldthwaite.

"I don't think they meant to be rude," said Elinor
Hadden. "I think they really felt badly; and that was
why it blurted right out so. They did n't know *what*
to say."

"Evidently," said Olivia. "And one does n't want
to be astonished in that way very often."

"I should n't mind having them," said Elinor, good-
naturedly. "They are kind-hearted people, and they
would feel hurt to be left out."

"That is just what stopped us," said Adelaide. "That
is just what the neighborhood is getting to be, — full of
people that you don't know what to do with."

" I don't see why we *need* to go out of our own set,"
said Olivia.

" O dear! O dear!"

It broke from Ruth involuntarily. Then she colored up,
as they all turned round upon her; but she was excited,
and Ruth's excitements made her forget that she was
Ruth, sometimes, for a moment. It had been growing in
her, from the beginning of the conversation; and now she
caught her breath, and felt her eyes light up. She turned
her face to Leslie Goldthwaite; but although she spoke
low she spoke somehow clearly, even more than she
meant, so that they all heard.

" What if the angels had said that before they came
down to Bethlehem!"

Then she knew by the hush that *she* had astonished
them, and she grew frightened; but she stood just so, and
would not let her look shrink; for she still felt just as she
did when the words came.

Mrs. Van Alstyne broke the pause with a good-natured
laugh.

" We can't go quite back to that, every time," she said.
" And we don't quite set up to be angels. Come, —
try one more round."

And with some of the hoops still hanging upon her arm,
she turned to pick up the others. Harry Goldthwaite of
course sprang forward to do it for her; and presently she
was tossing them with her peculiar grace, till the stake
was all wreathed with them from bottom to top, the last
hoop hanging itself upon the golden ball; a touch more
dexterous and consummate, it seemed, than if it had fairly
slidden over upon the rest.

Rosamond knew what a cunning and friendly turn it was; if it had not been for Mrs. Van Alstyne, Ruth's speech would have broken up the party. As it was, the game began again, and they stayed an hour longer.

Not all of them; for as soon as they were fairly engaged, Ruth said to Leslie Goldthwaite, "I must go now; I ought to have gone before. Reba will be waiting for me. Just tell them, if they ask."

But Leslie and the cadet walked away with her; slowly, across the grounds, so that she thought they were going back from the gate; but they kept on up over the hill.

"Was it very shocking?" asked Ruth, troubled in her

mind. "I could not help it; but I was frightened to death the next minute."

"About as frightened as the man is who stands to his gun in the front," said Dakie Thayne. "You never flinched."

"They would have thought it was from what I had said," Ruth answered. "And *that* was another thing from the *saying*."

"*You* had something to say, Leslie. It was just on the corner of your lip. I saw it."

"Yes; but Ruth said it all in one flash. It would have spoiled it if I had spoken then."

"I'm always sorry for people who don't know how," said Ruth. "I'm sure I don't know how myself so often."

"That is just it," said Leslie. "Why should n't these girls come up? And how will they ever, unless somebody overlooks? They would find out these mistakes in a little while, just as they find out fashions: picking up the right things from people who do know how. It is a kind of leaven, like greater good. And how can we stand anywhere in the lump, and say it shall not spread to the next particle?"

"They think it was pushing of them, to come here to live at all," said Ruth.

"Well, we're all pushing, if we're good for anything," said Leslie. "Why may n't they push, if they don't crowd out anybody else? It seems to me that the wrong sort of pushing is pushing down."

"Only there would be no end to it," said Dakie Thayne, "would there? There are coarse, vulgar people always, who are wanting to get in just for the sake of being in. What are the nice ones to do?"

"Just *be* nice, I think," said Leslie. "Nicer with those people than with anybody else even. If there were n't any difficulty made about it, — if there were n't any keeping out, — they would tire of the niceness probably sooner than anything. I don't suppose it is the fence that keeps out weeds."

"You are just like Mrs. Ingleside," said Ruth, walking closer to Leslie as she spoke.

"And Mrs. Ingleside is like Miss Craydocke; and — I did n't suppose I should ever find many more of them, but they 're counting up," said Dakie Thayne. "There 's a pretty good piece of the world salted, after all."

"If there really is any best society," pursued Leslie, "it seems to me it ought to be, not for keeping people out, but for getting everybody in as fast as it can, like the kingdom of heaven."

"Ah, but that *is* kingdom come," said Dakie Thayne.

It seemed as if the question of "things next" was to arise continually, in fresh shapes, just now, when things next for the Holabirds were nearer next than ever before.

"We must have Delia Waite again soon, if we can get her," said mother, one morning, when we were all quietly sitting in her room, and she was cutting out some shirts for Stephen. "All our changes and interruptions have put back the sewing so lately."

"We ought not to have been idle so much," said Barbara. "We 've been a family of grasshoppers all summer."

"Well, the grasshopping has done you all good. I 'm not sorry for it," said Mrs. Holabird. "Only we must have Delia for a week now, and be busy."

"If Delia Waite did n't have to come to our table!" said Rosamond.

" Why don't you try the girl Mrs. Hadden has, mother? She goes right into the kitchen with the other servants."

" I don't believe our ' other servants ' would know what to do with her," said Barbara. " There 's always such a crowd in our kitchen."

" Barbara, you 're a plague ! "

" Yes. I 'm the thorn in the flesh in this family, lest it should be exalted above measure ; and like Saint Paul, I magnify mine office."

" In the way we live," said Mrs. Holabird, " it is really more convenient to let a seamstress come right to table with us ; and besides, you know what I think about it. It is a little breath of life to a girl like that ; she gets something that we can give as well as not, and that helps her up. It comes naturally, as it cannot come with ' other servants.' She sits with us all day ; her work is among ladies, and with them ; she gets something so far, even in the midst of measurings and gorings, that common housemaids cannot get ; why should n't she be with us when we can leave off talk of measures and gores, and get what Ruth calls the ' very next ' ? Delia Waite is too nice a girl to be put into the kitchen to eat with Katty, in her ' crowd.' "

" But it seems to set us down ; it seems common in us to be so ready to be familiar with common people. More in us, because we do live plainly. If Mrs. Hadden or Mrs. Marchbanks did it, it might seem kind *without* the common. I think they ought to begin such things."

" But then if they don't ? Very likely it would be far more inconvenient for them ; and not the same good either, because it *would* be, or seem, a condescension.

We are the ' very next,' and we must be content to be the step we are."

"It 's the other thing with us, — con-*ascension*, — is n't it, mother? A step up for somebody, and no step down for anybody. Mrs. Ingleside does it," Ruth added.

"O, Mrs. Ingleside does all sorts of things. She has *that* sort of position. It 's as independent as the other. High moral and high social can do anything. It 's the betwixt and between that must be careful."

"What a miserably negative set we are, in such a positive state of the world!" cried Barbara. "Except Ruth's music, there is n't a specialty among us; we have n't any views; we 're on the mean-spirited side of the Woman Question; 'all woman, and no question,' as mother says; we shall never preach, nor speech, nor leech; we can't be magnificent, and we won't be common! I don't see what is to become of us, unless — and I wonder if maybe that is n't it? — we just do two or three rather right things in a no-particular sort of a way."

"Barbara, how nice you are!" cried Ruth.

"No. I 'm a thorn. Don't touch me."

"We never have company when we are having sewing done," said Mrs. Holabird. "We can always manage that."

"I don't want to play Box and Cox," said Rosamond.

"That 's the beauty of you, Rosa Mundi!" said Barbara, warmly. "You don't want to *play* anything. That 's where you 'll come out sun-clear and diamond-bright!"

CHAPTER V.

THE "BACK YETT AJEE."

HOSE who do not like common people need not read this chapter.

We had Delia Waite the next week. It happened well, in a sort of Box-and-Cox fashion; for Mrs. Van Alstyne went off with some friends to the Isles of Shoals, and Alice and Adelaide Marchbanks went with her; so that we knew we should see nothing of the two great families for a good many days; and when Leslie came, or the Haddens, we did not so much mind; besides, they knew that we were busy, and they did not expect any "coil" got up for them. Leslie came right up stairs, when she was alone; if Harry or Mr. Thayne were with her, one of us would take a wristband or a bit of ruffling, and go down. Somehow, if it happened to be Harry, Barbara was always tumultuously busy, and never offered to receive: but it always ended in Rosamond's **making her.** It seemed **to** be one of the things that people **wait to** be overcome **in** their objections to.

We always **had a snug, cosey time when Delia was with us;** we were all simple and busy, and the work was getting **on;** that was such **an** under-satisfaction; **and** Delia **was** having such a **good time.** She hardly ever failed **to come** to us when we **wanted her;** she could always make some arrangement.

Ruth was artful; **she** tucked in Lucilla Waters, **after all;** she **said it would be such** a nice chance **to have her; she knew she** would rather come **when we** were by **our- selves,** and especially **when we had our** work and patterns **about.** Lucilla brought **a sack and** an overskirt to make; **she could hardly have been spared if she** had **had to** bring **mere** idle work. She **sewed in** gathers **upon** the shirts for mother, while Delia **cut out her pretty** material in **a style** she had not seen. **If we had had grasshopper parties all** summer before, this **was certainly a bee·, and I** think **we** all really liked **it just as well as** the other.

We had the comfort of mother's great, **airy room, now,** as we had never even realized it before. Everybody had a window to sit at; green-shaded with closed blinds for **the** most part; but that is so beautiful in summer, when **the** out-of-doors comes brimming in with scent and sound, **and we know how glorious it is if we** choose to open to it, **and how glorious it is going to be when we do** throw all wide in **the cooling afternoon.**

"How glad **I** am we *have* **to have busy** weeks some- times!" said Ruth, stopping **the little** "common-sense" for **an** instant, while she tossed a long flouncing over her sewing-table. "I know now why people who never do their own work are obliged to go away from home for a change. It must be dreadfully same if they did n't. I like a book full of different stories ! "

Lucilla Waters lives down in the heart of the town. So does Leslie Goldthwaite, to be sure ; but then Mr. Goldthwaite's is one of the old, old-fashioned houses that were built when the town was country, and that has its great yard full of trees and flowers around it now ; and Mrs. Waters lives in a block, flat-face to the street, with nothing pretty outside, and not very much in ; for they have never been rich, the Waterses, and Mr. Waters died ten years ago, when Lucilla was a little child. Lucilla and her mother keep a little children's school ; but it was vacation now, of course.

Lucilla is in Mrs. Ingleside's Bible-class ; that is how Ruth, and then the rest of us, came to know her. Arctura Fish is another of Mrs. Ingleside's scholars. She is a poor girl, living at service, — or, rather, working in a family for board, clothing, and a little " schooling," — the best of which last she gets on Sundays of Mrs. Ingleside, — until she shall have " learned how," and be " worth wages."

Arctura Fish is making herself up, slowly, after the pattern of Lucilla Waters. She would not undertake Leslie Goldthwaite or Helen Josselyn, — Mrs. Ingleside's younger sister, who stays with her so much, — or even our quiet Ruth. But Lucilla Waters comes *just next*. She can just reach up to her. She can see how she does up her hair, in something approaching the new way, lean-ing back behind her in the class and tracing out the twists between the questions ; for Lucilla can only afford to use her own, and a few strands of harmless **Berlin wool** under it; she can't buy coils and braids and two-dollar **rats,** or intricacies **ready made** up at the — upholsterer's, I was going to say. So it is not a hopeless puzzle and an impracticable achievement to little Arctura Fish. It is wonderful how **nice she has made** herself look lately, and how many little **ways she puts on, just** like Lucilla's. She has n't got beyond mere mechanical copying, yet; when she reaches to where Lucilla really is, she will take in differently.

Ruth gave up her little white **room** to Delia Waite, and went to sleep with Lucilla in the great, square east room.

Delia Waite thought a great deal of this; and it was wonderful how nobody could ever get a peep at the room when it looked as if anything in it had been used or touched. Ruth is pretty nice about it; but she cannot keep it so *sacredly* fair and pure as Delia did for her. Only one thing showed.

"I say," said Stephen, one morning, sliding by Ruth on the stair-rail as they came down to breakfast, "do you look after that *piousosity,* now, mornings?"

"No," said Ruth, laughing, "of course I can't."

"It's always whopped," said Stephen, sententiously.

Barbara got up some of her special cookery in these days. Not her very finest, out of Miss Leslie; she said that was too much like the fox and the crane, when Lucilla asked for the receipts. It was n't fair to give a taste of things that we ourselves could only have for very best, and send people home to wish for them. But she made some of her "griddles trimmed with lace," as only Barbara's griddles were trimmed; the brown lightness run-

ning out at the edges into crisp filigree. And another
time it was the flaky spider-cake, turned just as it blushed
golden-tawny over the coals; and then it was breakfast
potato, beaten almost frothy with one white-of-egg, a
pretty good bit of butter, a few spoonfuls of top-of-the-
milk, and seasoned plentifully with salt, and delicately
with pepper, — the oven doing the rest, and turning it
into a snowy soufflé.

Barbara said we had none of us a specialty; she knew
better; only hers was a very womanly and old-fashioned,
not to say kitcheny one; and would be quite at a discount
when the grand co-operative kitchens should come into
play; for who cares to put one's genius into the universal
and indiscriminate mouth, or make potato-soufflés to be
carried half a mile to the table?

Barbara delighted to "make company" of seamstress
week; "it was so nice," she said, "to entertain somebody who thought ' chickings was 'evingly.' "

Rosamond liked that part of it; she enjoyed giving
pleasure no less than any; but she had a secret misgiving
that we were being very vulgarly comfortable in an underhand way. She would never, by any means, go off by
herself to eat with her fingers.

Delia Waite said she never came to our house that she
did not get some new ideas to carry home to Arabel.

Arabel Waite was fifty years old, or more; she was
the oldest child of one marriage and Delia the youngest
of another. All the Waites between them had dropped
away, — out of the world, or into homes here and there
of their own, — and Arabel and Delia were left together
in the square, low, gambrel-roofed house over on the other
hill, where the town ran up small.

Arabel Waite was an old dressmaker. She *could* make two skirts to a dress, one shorter, the other longer; and she could cut out the upper one by any new paper pattern; and she could make shell-trimmings and flutings and box-plaitings and flouncings, and sew them on exquisitely, even now, with her old eyes; but she never had adapted herself to the modern ideas of the corsage. She could not fit a bias to save her life; she could only stitch up a straight slant, and leave the rest to nature and fate. So all her people had the squarest of wooden fronts, and were preternaturally large around the waist. Delia sewed with her, abroad and at home, — abroad without her, also, as she was doing now for us. A pattern for a sleeve, or a cape, or a panier, — or a receipt for a tea-biscuit or a johnny-cake, was something to go home with rejoicing.

Arabel Waite and Delia could only use three rooms of the old house; the rest was blinded and shut up; the garret was given over to the squirrels, who came in from the great butternut-trees in the yard, and stowed away their rich provision under the eaves and away down between the walls, and grew fat there all winter, and frolicked like a troop of horse. We liked to hear Delia tell of their pranks, and of all the other queer, quaint things in their way of living. Everybody has a way of living; and if you can get into it, every one is as good as a story. It always seemed to us as if Delia brought with her the atmosphere of mysterious old houses, and old, old books stowed away in their by-places, and stories of the far past that had been lived there, and curious ancient garments done with long ago, and packed into trunks and bureaus

6

in the dark, unused rooms, where there had been parties
once, and weddings and funerals and children's games **in**
nurseries ; and strange fellowship of little wild things that
strayed in now, — bees in summer, and squirrels in winter, — and brought the woods and fields with them under
the old roof. Why, I think we should have missed it
more than she would, if we had put her into some back
room, and poked her sewing in at her, and left her **to her-**
self !

The only thing that was n't nice that week was Aunt
Roderick coming over one morning in the very thick of
our work, and Lucilla's too, walking straight up stairs, as
aunts can, whether you want them or not, and standing
astonished at the great goings-on.

" Well ! " she exclaimed, with a strong falling inflection,
" are any of you getting ready to be married ? "

" Yes 'm," said Barbara, gravely, handing her a chair.
" All of us."

Then Barbara made rather an unnecessary parade of
ribbon that she was quilling up, and of black lace that was
to go each side of it upon a little round jacket for her blue
silk dress, made **of a piece** laid away five **years ago, when**
she first had **it.   The skirt was turned now, and** the waist
was gone.

While Aunt **Roderick was** there, she also took occasion
to toss over, more or less, everything that lay about, —
" to help her in her inventory," she said after she went
away.

" Twelve new embroidered cambric handkerchiefs,"
repeated **she, as** she turned back **from the** stair-head,
having **seen Aunt Roderick down.**

Barbara had once, in a severe fit of needle-industry, inspired by the discovery of two baby robes of linen cambric among mother's old treasures, and their bestowal upon her, turned them into these elegances, broadly hemmed with the finest machine stitch, and marked with beautiful great B's in the corners. She showed them, in her pride, to Mrs. Roderick ; and we knew afterward what her abstract report had been, in Grandfather Holabird's hearing. Grandfather Holabird knew we did without a good many things ; but he had an impression of us, from instances like these, that we were seized with sudden spasms of recklessness at times, and rushed into French embroideries and sets of jewelry. I believe he heard of mother's one handsome black silk, every time she wore it upon semiannual occasions, until he would have said that Mrs. Stephen had a new fifty-dollar dress every six months. This was one of our little family trials.

"I don't think Mrs. Roderick does it on purpose," Ruth would say. "I think there are two things that make her talk in that way. In the first place, she has got into the habit of carrying home all the news she can, and making it as big as possible, to amuse Mr. Holabird ; and then she has to settle it over in her own mind, every once in a while, that things must be pretty comfortable amongst us, down here, after all."

Ruth never dreamed of being satirical ; it was a perfectly straightforward explanation ; and it showed, she truly believed, two quite kind and considerate points in Aunt Roderick's character.

After the party came back from the Isles of Shoals,

Mrs. Van Alstyne went down to Newport. The March
bankses had other visitors, — people whom we did not
know, and in whose way we were not thrown; the *haute
volée* was sufficient to itself again, and we lived on a piece
of our own life once more.

"It's rather nice to knit on straight," said Barbara; "without any widening or narrowing or counting of stitches. I like very well to come to a plain
place."

Rosamond never liked the plain places quite so much;
but she accommodated herself beautifully, and was just as
nice as she could be. And the very best thing about
Rose was, that she never put on anything, or left anything off, of her gentle ways and notions. She would
have been ready at any time for the most delicate fancy-
pattern that could be woven upon her plain places. That
was one thing which mother taught us all.

"Your life will come to you; you need not run after
it," she would say, if we ever got restless and began to
think there was no way out of the family hedge. "Have
everything in yourselves as it should be, and then you can
take the chances as they arrive."

"Only we need n't put our bonnets on, and sit at the
windows," Barbara once replied.

"No," said Mrs. Holabird; "and especially at the
front windows. A great deal that is good — a great deal
of the best — comes in at the back-doors."

Everybody, we thought, did not have a back-door to
their life, as we did. They hardly seemed to know if they
had one to their houses.

Our "back yett was ajee," now, at any rate.

Leslie Goldthwaite came in at it, though, just the same, and so did her cousin and Dakie.*

Otherwise, for two or three weeks, our chief variety was in sending for old Miss Trixie Spring to spend the day.

Miss Trixie Spring is a lively old lady, who, some threescore and five years ago, was christened " Beatrix." She plays backgammon in the twilights, with mother, and makes a table at whist, at once lively and severe, in the evenings, for father. At this whist-table, Barbara usually is the fourth. Rosamond gets sleepy over it, and Ruth — Miss Trixie says — " plays like a ninkum."

We always wanted Miss Trixie, somehow, to complete comfort, when we were especially comfortable by ourselves ; when we had something particularly good for dinner, or found ourselves set cheerily down for a long day at quiet work, with everything early-nice about us ; or when we were going to make something " contrive-y," " Swiss-family-Robinson-ish," that got us all together over it, in the hilarity of enterprise and the zeal of acquisition. Miss Trixie could appreciate homely cleverness ; darning of carpets and covering of old furniture ; she could darn a carpet herself, so as almost to improve upon — certainly to supplant — the original pattern. Yet she always had a fresh amazement for all our performances, as if nothing notable had ever been done before, and a personal delight in every one of our improvements, as if they had been her own.

" We're just as cosey as we can be, already, — it is n't that ; but we want somebody to tell us how cosey we are. Let 's get Miss Trixie to-day," says Barbara.

---

* Harry Goldthwaite is Leslie's cousin, and Mr. Aaron Goldthwaite's ward. I do not believe we have ever thought to put this in before.

Once was when the new drugget went down, at last, **in the** dining-room. It was tan-color, bound with crimson, — covering three square yards ; and mother nailed it down with brass-headed tacks, right after breakfast, one cool morning. Then Katty washed up the dark floor-margin, and the table had its crimson-striped cloth on, and mother brought down the brown stuff for **the** new **sofa-**cover, and the great bunch of crimson braid to bind that with, and we drew up our camp-chairs **and** crickets, and got ready to be busy **and** jolly, **and** to have a brand-new **piece** of furniture before night.

Barbara had made peach-dumpling for dinner, and of **course** Aunt Trixie was the last and crowning suggestion. **It was** not far to send, and she was not long in coming, with her second-best cap pinned **up** in a handkerchief, and her knitting-work and her spectacles in her bag.

The Marchbankses never made sofa-covers of brown waterproof, nor had Miss Trixies to spend the day. That was because they had no back-door to their house.

I suppose you think there are a good many people in our story. There are ; when we think it **up** there are ever so many people that have **to** do **with our story** every day ; but we don't mean to tell you **all** *their* **stories ;** so you can **bear** with the momentary **introduction** when you meet **them in** our brown **room, or in our** dining-room, of a morning, although we know very well also that passing introductions are going out of fashion.

We had Dakie Thayne's last visit that day, in the midst **of** the hammering and binding. Leslie and he came in with Ruth, when she came back from her hour **with** Reba Hadden. It was to bid us good by ; his furlough was over; he was **to return to** West Point on **Monday.**

"Another two years' pull," he said. "Won't you all come to West Point next summer?"

"If we take the journey we think of," said Barbara, composedly,—"to the mountains and Montreal and Quebec; perhaps up the Saguenay; and then back, up Lake Champlain, and down the Hudson, on our way to Saratoga and Niagara. We might keep on to West Point first, and have a day or two there."

"Barbara," said mother, remonstratingly.

"Why? *Don't* we think of it? I'm sure I do. I've thought of it till I'm almost tired of it. I don't much believe we shall come, after all, Mr. Thayne."

"We shall miss you very much," said Mrs. Holabird, covering Barbara's nonsense.

"Our summer has stopped right in the middle," said Barbara, determined to talk.

"I shall hear about you all," said Dakie Thayne. "There's to be a Westover column in Leslie's news. I wish —" and there the cadet stopped.

Mother looked up at him with a pleasant inquiry.

"I was going to say, I wish there might be a Westover correspondent, to put in just a word or two, sometimes; but then I was afraid that would be impertinent. When a fellow has only eight weeks in the year of living, Mrs. Holabird, and all the rest is drill, you don't know how he hangs on to those eight weeks, — and how they hang on to him afterwards."

Mother looked so motherly at him then !

"We shall not forget you — Dakie," she said, using his first name for the first time. "You shall have a message from us now and then."

Dakie said, "Thank you," in a tone that responded to her "Dakie."

We all knew he liked Mrs. Holabird ever so much. Homes and mothers are beautiful things to boys who have had to do without them.

He shook hands with us all round, when he got up to go. He shook hands also with our old friend, Miss Trixie, whom he had never happened to see before. Then Rosamond went out with him and Leslie, — as it was our cordial, countrified fashion for somebody to do, — through the hall to the door. Ruth went as far as the stairs, on her way to her room to take off her things. She stood there, up two steps, as they were leaving.

Dakie Thayne said good by again to Rosamond, at the door, as was natural; and then he came quite back, and said it last of all, once more, to little Ruth upon the stairs. He certainly did hate to go away and leave us all.

"That is a very remarkable pretty-behaved young man," said Miss Trixie, when we all picked up our breadths of waterproof, and got in behind them again.

"The world is a desert, and the sand has got into my eyes," said Barbara, who had hushed up ever since mother had said "Dakie." When anybody came close to mother, Barbara was touched. I think her love for mother is more like a son's than a daughter's, in the sort of chivalry it has with it.

It was curious how suddenly our little accession of social importance had come on, and wonderful how quickly it had subsided; more curious and wonderful still, how entirely it seemed to stay subsided.

We had plenty to do, though; we did not miss anything; only we had quite taken up with another set of things. This was the way it was with us; we had things we *must* take up; we could not have spared time to lead society for a long while together.

Aunt Roderick claimed us, too, in our leisure hours, just then; she had a niece come to stay with her; and we had to go over to the "old house" and spend afternoons, and ask Aunt Roderick and Miss Bragdowne in to tea with us. Aunt Roderick always expected this sort of attention; and yet she had a way with her as if we ought not to try to afford things, looked scrutinizingly at the quality of our cake and preserves, and seemed to eat our bread and butter with consideration.

It helped Rosamond very much, though, over the tran-
sition.   We, also, had had private occupation.

"There had been family company at grandfather's,"
she told Jeannie Hadden, one morning.   "We had been
very much engaged among ourselves. We had hardly
seen anything of the other girls for two or three weeks."

Barbara sat at the round table, where Stephen had been
doing his geometry last night, twirling a pair of pencil
compasses about on a sheet of paper, while this was saying.   She lifted up her eyes a little, cornerwise, without
moving her head, and gave a twinkle of mischief over at
mother and Ruth.   When Jeannie was gone, she kept on
silently, a few minutes, with her diagrams.   Then she
said, in her funniest, repressed way, —

"I can see a little how it must be ; but I suppose I
ought to understand the differential calculus to compute
it.   Circles are wonderful things ; and the science of
curves holds almost everything.   Rose, when do you
think we shall get round again ? "

She held up her bit of paper as she spoke, scrawled
over with intersecting circles and arcs and ellipses, against
whose curves and circumferences she had written names :
Marchbanks, Hadden, Goldthwaite, Holabird.

"It 's a mere question of centre and radius," she said.
"You may be big enough to take in the whole of them,
or you may only cut in at the sides.   You may be just
tangent for a minute, and then go off into space on your
own account.   You may have your centre barely inside
of a great ring, and yet reach pretty well out of it for a
good part ; you must be small to be taken quite in by
anybody's ! "

"It does n't illustrate," said Rose, coolly. "Orbits don't snarl up in that fashion."

"Geometry does," said Barbara. "I told you I could n't work it all out. But I suppose there 's a Q. E. D. at the end of it somewhere."

Two or three days after something new happened; an old thing happened freshly, rather, — which also had to do with our orbit and its eccentricities. Barbara, as usual, discovered and announced it.

"I should think *any* kind of an astronomer might be mad!" she exclaimed. "Periods and distances are bad enough; but then come the perturbations! Here 's one. We 're used to it, to be sure; but we never know exactly where it may come in. The girl we live with has formed other views for herself, and is going off at a tangent. What *is* the reason we can't keep a satellite, — planet, I mean?"

"Barbara!" said mother, anxiously, "don't be absurd!"

"Well, what shall I be? We 're all out of a place again." And she sat down resignedly on a very low cricket, in the middle of the room.

"I 'll tell you what we 'll do, mother," said Ruth, coming round. "I 've thought of it this good while. We 'll co-operate!"

"She 's glad of it! She 's been waiting for a chance! I believe she put the luminary up to it! Ruth, you 're a brick — moon!"

CHAPTER VI.

CO-OPERATING.

HEN mother first read that arti‑
cle in the Atlantic she had said,
right off, —

"I 'm sure I wish they
would ! "

" Would what, mother ? "
asked Barbara.

" Co-operate."

" O mother ! I really do be‑
lieve you must belong, some‑
how, to the Micawber family !
I should n't wonder if one of
these days, when they come into
their luck, you should hear of
something greatly to your ad‑
vantage, from over the water.
You have such faith in ' they ' !
I don't believe ' *they* ' will ever
do much for ' *us* ' ! "

" What is it, dear ? " asked Mrs. Hobart, rousing from
a little arm-chair wink, during which Mrs. Holabird had
taken up the magazine.

Mrs. Hobart had come in, with her cable wool and her
great ivory knitting-pins, to sit an hour, sociably.

"Co-operative housekeeping, ma'am," said Barbara.

"Oh! Yes. That is what they *used* to have, in old times, when we lived at home with mother. Only they did n't write articles about it. All the women in a house co-operated — to keep it; and all the neighborhood co-operated — by living exactly in the same way. Nowadays, it 's co-operative shirking; is n't it?"

One never could quite tell whether Mrs. Hobart was more simple or sharp.

That was all that was said about co-operative housekeeping at the time. But Ruth remembered the conversation. So did Barbara, for a while, as appeared in something she came out with a few days after.

"I could — almost — write a little poem!" she said, suddenly, over her work. "Only that would be doing just what the rest do. Everything turns into a poem, or an article, nowadays. I wish we 'd lived in the times when people *did* the things!"

"O Barbara! *Think* of all that is being done in the world!"

"I know. But the little private things. They want to turn everything into a movement. Miss Trixie says they won't have any eggs from their fowls next winter; all their chickens are roosters, and all they 'll do will be to sit in a row on the fence and crow! I think the world is running pretty much to roosters."

"Is that the poem?"

"I don't know. It might come in. All I 've got is the end of it. It came into my head hind side before. If it could only have a beginning and a middle put to it, it might do. It 's just the wind-up, where they have to give an account, you know, and what they 'll have to show for it, and the thing that really amounts, after all."

" Well, tell us."

" It 's only five lines, and one rhyme. But it might be written up to. They could say all sorts of things, — one and another : —

> " *I* wrote some little books ;
> *I* said some little **says** ;
> *I* preached a little preach ;
> *I* lit a little blaze ;
> *I* made things pleasant in one little place."

There was a shout at Barbara's " poem."

" I thought I might as well relieve my mind," she said, meekly. " I knew it was all there would **ever** be of it."

But Barbara's **rhyme** stayed in our heads, and got quoted in the family. She illustrated on a small scale what the " poems and articles " *may* sometimes do in the great world.

We remembered it that day when Ruth said, " Let 's co-operate."

We talked it over, — what we could do without a girl. We had talked it over before. We had had to try it, more or less, during interregnums. But in our little house in Z——, with the dark kitchen, and with Barbara and Ruth going to school, and the washing-days, when we had to hire, it always cost more than it came to, besides making what Barb called a " heave-offering of life."

" They used to have houses built accordingly," Rosamond said, speaking of the " old times." " Grandmother's kitchen was the biggest and pleasantest room in the house."

" Could n't we *make* the kitchen the pleasantest room ? " suggested Ruth. " Would n't it be sure to be, if it was the room we all stayed in mornings, and where we had our morning work ? Whatever room we do that in always is, you know. The look grows. Kitchens are horrid when girls have just gone out of them, and left the dish-towels dirty, and the dish-cloth all wabbled up in the sink, and all the tins and irons wanting to be cleaned. But if we once got up a real ladies' kitchen of our own ! I can think how it might be lovely ! "

" I can think how it might be jolly-nificent ! " cried Barbara, relapsing into her dislocations.

" *You* like kitchens," said Rosamond, in a tone of quiet ill-usedness.

" Yes, I do," said Barbara. " And you like parlors, and prettinesses, and feather dusters, and little general touch-ings-up, that I can't have patience with. You shall take the high art, and I 'll have the low realities. That 's the co-operation. Families are put up assorted, and the home character comes of it. It 's Bible-truth, you know ; the head and the feet and the eye and the hand, and all that. Let 's just see what we *shall* come to ! People don't turn out what they 're meant, who have Irish kitchens and high-style parlors, all alike. There 's a great deal in being Holabirdy, — or whatever-else-you-are-y ! "

" If it only were n't for that cellar-kitchen," said Mrs. Holabird.

" Mother," said Ruth, " what if we were to take this ? " We were in the dining-room.

" This nice room ! "

" It is to be a ladies' kitchen, you know."

Everybody glanced around.   It was nice, ever so nice. The dark-stained floor, showing clean, undefaced margins, — the new, pretty drugget, — the freshly clad, broad old sofa, — the high wainscoted walls, painted in oak and walnut colors, and varnished brightly, — the ceiling faintly tinted with buff, — the buff holland shades to the windows, — the dresser-closet built out into the room on one side, with its glass upper-halves to the doors, showing our prettiest china and a gleam of silver and glass, — the two or three pretty engravings in the few spaces for them, — O, it was a great deal too nice to take for a kitchen.

But Ruth began again.

" You know, mother, before Katty came, how nice everything was down stairs.   We cooked nearly a fortnight, and washed dishes, and everything; and we only had the floor scrubbed once, and there never was a slop on the stove, or a teaspoonful of anything spilled.   It would be so different from a girl !   It seems as if we *might* bring the kitchen up stairs, instead of going down into the kitchen."

" But the stove," said mother.

" I think," said Barbara, boldly, " that a cooking-stove, all polished up, is just as handsome a thing as there is in a house ! "

" It is clumsy, one must own," said Mrs. Holabird, " besides being suggestive."

" So is a piano," said the determined Barbara.

" I can *imagine* a cooking-stove," said Rosamond, slowly.

" Well, do ! That's just where your gift will come in ! "

" A pretty copper tea-kettle, and a shiny tin boiler, made

to order, — like an urn, or something, — with a copper faucet, and nothing else ever about, except it were that minute wanted; and all the tins and irons begun with new again, and kept clean; and little cocoanut dippers with German silver rims ; and things generally contrived as they are for other kinds of rooms that ladies use ; it *might* be like that little picnicking dower-house we read about in a novel, or like Marie Antoinette's Trianon."

"That's what it *would* come to, if it was part of our living, just as we come to have gold thimbles and lovely work-boxes. We should give each other Christmas and birthday presents of things ; we should have as much pleasure and pride in it as in the china-closet. Why, the whole trouble is that the kitchen is the only place taste *has n't* got into. Let's have an art-kitchen ! "

"We might spend a little money in fitting up a few things freshly, if we are to save the waste and expense of a servant," said Mrs. Holabird.

The idea grew and developed.

"But when we have people to tea ! " Rosamond said, suddenly demurring afresh.

"There's always the brown room, and the handing round," said Barbara, " for the people you can't be intimate with, and *think* how crowsy this will be with Aunt Trixie or Mrs. Hobart or the Goldthwaites!"

"We shall just settle *down*," said Rose, gloomily.

"Well, I believe in finding our place. Every little brook runs till it does that. I don't want to stand on tiptoe all my life."

"We shall always gather to us what *belongs*. Every

7

little crystal does that," said mother, taking up another simile.

"What will Aunt Roderick say?" said Ruth.

"I shall keep her out of the kitchen, and tell her we could n't manage with one girl any longer, and so we 've taken three that all wanted to get a place together."

And Barbara actually did; and it was three weeks before Mrs. Roderick found out what it really meant.

We were in a hurry to have Katty go, and to begin, after we had made up our minds; and it was with the serenest composure that Mrs. Holabird received her remark that "her week would be up a-Tuesday, an' she hoped agin then we 'd be shooted wid a girl."

"Yes, Katty; I am ready at any moment," was the reply; which caused the whites of Katty's eyes to appear for a second between the lids and the irids.

There had been only one applicant for the place, who had come while we had not quite irrevocably fixed our plans.

Mother swerved for a moment; she came in and told us what the girl said.

"She is not experienced; but she looks good-natured; and she is willing to come for a trial."

"They all do that," said Barbara, gravely. "I think — as Protestants — we 've hired enough of them."

Mother laughed, and let the "trial" go. That was the end, I think, of our indecisions.

We got Mrs. Dunikin to come and scrub; we pulled out pots and pans, stove-polish and dish-towels, napkins and odd stockings missed from the wash; we cleared every corner, and had every box and bottle washed; then we left everything below spick and span, so that it almost tempted us to stay even there, and sent for the sheet-iron man, and had the stove taken up stairs. We only carried up such lesser movables as we knew we should want; we left all the accumulation behind; we resolved to begin life anew, and feel our way, and furnish as we went along.

Ruth brought home a lovely little spice-box as the first donation to the art-kitchen. Father bought a copper tea-kettle, and the sheet-iron man made the tin boiler. There was a wide, high, open fireplace in the dining-room; we had wondered what we should do with it in the winter. It had a soapstone mantel, with fluted pilasters, and a brown-stone hearth and jambs. Back a little, between these sloping jambs, we had a nice iron fire-board set, with an ornamental collar around the funnel-hole. The stove stood modestly sheltered, as it were, in its new position, its features softened to almost a sitting-room congruity; it did not thrust itself obtrusively forward, and force its homely association upon you; it was low, too, and its broad top looked smooth and enticing.

There was a large, light closet at the back of the room, where was set a broad, deep iron sink, and a pump came up from the cistern. This closet had double sliding doors; it could be thrown all open for busy use, or closed quite away and done with.

There were shelves here, and cupboards. Here we ranged our tins and our saucepans, — the best and newest; Rosamond would have nothing to do with the old battered ones; over them we hung our spoons and our little strainers, our egg-beaters, spatulas, and quart measures, — these last polished to the brightness of silver tank-

ards; in one corner stood the flour-barrel, and over it
was the sieve; in the cupboards were our porcelain kettles, — we bought two new ones, a little and a big, — the
frying-pans, delicately smooth and nice now, outside and
in, the roasting-pans, and the one iron pot, which we
never meant to use when we could help it. The worst
things we could have to wash were the frying and roast-
ing pans, and these, we soon found, were not bad when
you did it all over and at once every time.

Adjoining this closet was what had been the "girl's
room," opening into the passage where the kitchen stairs

came up; and the passage itself was fair-sized and square, corresponding to the depth of the other divisions. Here we had a great box placed for wood, and a barrel for coal, and another for kindlings; once a week these could be replenished as required, when the man came who "chored" for us. The "girl's room" would be a spare place that we should find twenty uses for; it was nice to think of it sweet and fresh, empty and available; very nice not to be afraid to remember it was there at all.

We had a Robinson-Crusoe-like pleasure in making all these arrangements; every clean thing that we put in a spotless place upon shelf or nail was a wealth and a comfort to us. Besides, we really did not need half the lumber of a common kitchen closet; a china bowl or plate would no longer be contraband of war, and Barbara said she could stir her blanc-mange with a silver spoon without demoralizing anybody to the extent of having the ashes taken up with it.

By Friday night we had got everything to the exact and perfect starting-point; and Mrs. Dunikin went home enriched with gifts that were to her like a tin-and-wooden wedding; we felt, on our part, that we had celebrated ours by clearing them out.

The bread-box was sweet and empty; the fragments had been all daintily crumbled by Ruth, as she sat, resting and talking, when she had come in from her music-lesson; they lay heaped up like lightly fallen snow, in a broad dish, ready to be browned for chicken dressing or boiled for brewis or a pudding. Mother never has anything between loaves and crumbs when *she* manages; then all is nice, and keeps nice.

"Clean beginnings are beautiful," said Rosamond, looking around. "It is the middle that's horrid."

"We won't have any middles," said Ruth. "We'll
keep making clean beginnings, all the way along. That
is the difference between work and muss."

"If you can," said Rose, doubtfully.

I suppose that is what some people will say, after this
Holabird story is printed so far. Then we just wish they
could have seen mother make a pudding or get a breakfast, that is all. A lady will no more make a jumble or
litter in doing such things than she would at her dressing-
table. It only needs an accustomed and delicate touch.

I will tell you something of how it was. I will take
that Monday morning — and Monday morning is as good,
for badness, as you can take — just after we had begun.

The room was nice enough for breakfast when we left
it over night. There was nothing straying about; the
tea-kettle and the tin boiler were filled, — father did that
just before he locked up the house; we had only to draw
up the window-shades, and let the sweet light in, in the
morning.

Stephen had put a basket of wood and kindlings ready
for Mrs. Dunikin in the kitchen below, and the key of the
lower door had been left on a beam in the woodshed, by
agreement. By the time we came down stairs Mrs. Dunikin had a steaming boiler full of clothes, and had done
nearly two of her five hours' work. We should hand her
her breakfast on a little tray, when the time came, at the
stair-head; and she would bring up her cup and plate
again while we were clearing away. We should pay her
twelve and a half cents an hour; she would scrub up all

below, go home to dinner, and come again to-morrow for five hours' ironing. That was all there would be about Mrs. Dunikin.

Meanwhile, with a pair of gloves on, and a little plain-hemmed three-cornered, dotted-muslin cap tied over her hair with a muslin bow behind, mother had let down the ashes, — it is n't a bad thing to do with a well-contrived stove, — and set the pan, to which we had a duplicate, into the out-room, for Stephen to carry away. Then into the clean grate went a handful of shavings and pitch-pine kindlings, one or two bits of hard wood, and a sprinkle of small, shiny nut-coal. The draughts were put on, and in five minutes the coals were red. In these five minutes the stove and the mantel were dusted, the hearth brushed up, and there was neither chip nor mote to tell the tale. It was not like an Irish fire, that reaches out into the middle of the room with its volcanic margin of cinders and ashes.

Then — that Monday morning — we had brewis to make, a little buttered toast to do, and some eggs to scramble. The bright coffee-pot got its ration of fragrant, beaten paste, — the brown ground kernels mixed with an egg, — and stood waiting for its drink of boiling water. The two frying-pans came forth ; one was set on with the milk for the brewis, into which, when it boiled up white and drifting, went the sweet fresh butter, and the salt, each in plentiful proportion ; — " one can give one's self carte-blancher," Barbara said, " than it will do to give a girl " ; — and then the bread-crumbs ; and the end of it was, in a white porcelain dish, a light, delicate, savory bread-porridge, to eat daintily with a fork, and be thankful for. The other pan held eggs, broken in upon bits of butter, and sprinkles of pepper and salt; this went on when the coffee-pot — which had got its drink when the milk boiled, and been puffing ever since — was ready to come off; over it stood Barbara with a tin spoon, to toss up and turn until the whole was just curdled with the heat into white and yellow flakes, not one of which was raw, nor one was dry. Then the two pans and the coffee-pot and the little bowl in which the coffee-paste had been beaten and the spoons went off into the pantry-closet, and the breakfast was ready; and only Barbara waited a moment to toast and butter the bread, while mother, in her place at table, was serving the cups. It was Ruth who had set the table, and carried off the cookery things, and folded and slid back the little pembroke, that had held them beside the stove, into its corner.

Rosamond had been busy in the brown room; that was all nice now for the day; and she came in with a little glass vase in her hand, in which was a tea-rose, that she put before mother at the edge of the white waiter-napkin; and it graced and freshened all the place; and the smell of it, and the bright September air that came in at the three cool west windows, overbore all remembrance of the cooking and reminder of the stove, from which we were seated well away, and before which stood now a square, dark green screen that Rosamond had recollected and brought down from the garret on Saturday. Barbara and her toast emerged from its shelter as innocent of behind-the-scenes as any bit of pretty play or pageant.

Barbara looked very nice this morning, in her brown-plaid Scotch gingham trimmed with white braids; she had brown slippers, also, with bows; she would not verify Rosamond's prophecy that she "would be all points," now that there was an apology for them. I think we were all more particular about our outer ladyhood than usual.

After breakfast the little pembroke was wheeled out again, and on it put a steaming pan of hot water. Ruth picked up the dishes; it was something really delicate to see her scrape them clean, with a pliant knife, as a painter might cleanse his palette, — we had, in fact, a palette-knife that we kept for this use when we washed our own dishes, — and then set them in piles and groups before mother, on the pembroke-table. Mother sat in her raised arm-chair, as she might sit making tea for company; she had her little mop, and three long, soft clean towels lay beside her; we had hemmed a new dozen, so as to have plenty from day to day, and a grand Dunikin wash at the end on the Mondays.

After the china and glass were done and put up, came forth the coffee-pot and the two pans, and had their scald, and their little scour, — a teaspoonful of sand must go to the daily cleansing of an iron utensil, in mother's hands; and *that* was clean work, and the iron thing never got to be "horrid," any more than a china bowl. It was only a little heavy, and it was black; but the black did not come off. It is slopping and burning and putting away with a rinse, that makes kettles and spiders untouchable. Besides, mother keeps a bottle of ammonia in the pantry, to qualify her soap and water with, when she comes to things like these. She calls it her kitchen-maid; it does wonders for any little roughness or greasiness; such soil comes off in that, and chemically disappears.

It was all dining-room work ; and we were chatty over
it, as if we had sat down to wind worsteds ; and there was
no kitchen in the house that morning.

We kept our butter and milk in the brick buttery at
the foot of the kitchen stairs.   These were all we had to
go up and down for.   Barbara set away the milk, and
skimmed the cream, and brought up and scalded the yesterday's pans the first thing ; and they were out in a row —
flashing up saucily at the sun and giving as good as he
sent — on the back platform.

She and Rosamond were up stairs, making beds and
setting straight ; and in an hour after breakfast the house
was in its beautiful forenoon order, and there was a forenoon of three hours to come.

We had chickens for dinner that day, I remember ; one
always does remember what was for dinner the first day
in a new house, or in new housekeeping.   William, the
chore-man, had killed and picked and drawn them, on
Saturday ; I do not mean to disguise that we avoided these
last processes ; we preferred a little foresight of arrangement.   They were hanging in the buttery, with their hearts
and livers inside them ; mother does not believe in gizzards.
They only wanted a little salt bath before cooking.

I should like to have had you see Mrs. Holabird tie up
those chickens.   They were as white and nice as her own
hands ; and their legs and wings were fastened down to
their sides, so that they were as round and comfortable
as dumplings before she had done with them ; and she
laid them out of her two little palms into the pan in a
cunning and cosey way that gave them a relish beforehand,
and sublimated the vulgar need.

We were tired of sewing and writing and reading in three hours; it was only restful change to come down and put the chickens into the oven, and set the dinner-table.

Then, in the broken hour while they were cooking, we drifted out upon the piazza, and among our plants in the shady east corner by the parlor windows, and Ruth played a little, and mother took up the Atlantic, and we felt we had a good right to the between-times when the fresh dredgings of flour were getting their brown, and after that, while the potatoes were boiling.

Barbara gave us currant-jelly; she was a stingy Barbara about that jelly, and counted her jars; and when father and Stephen came in, there was the little dinner of three covers, and a peach-pie of Saturday's making on the side-board, and the green screen up before the stove again, and the baking-pan safe in the pantry sink, with hot water and ammonia in it.

"Mother," said Barbara, "I feel as if we had got rid of a menagerie!"

"It is the girl that makes the kitchen," said Ruth.

"And then the kitchen that has to have the girl," said Mrs. Holabird.

Ruth got up and took away the dishes, and went round with the crumb-knife, and did not forget to fill the tumblers, nor to put on father's cheese.

Our talk went on, and we forgot there was any "tending."

"We did n't feel all that in the ends of our elbows," said mother in a low tone, smiling upon Ruth as she sat down beside her.

"Nor have to scrinch all up," said Stephen, quite out loud, "for fear she 'd touch us!"

I 'll tell you — in confidence — another of our ways at Westover; what we did, mostly, after the last two meals, to save our afternoons and evenings and our nice dresses. We always did it with the tea-things. We just put them, neatly piled and ranged in that deep pantry sink; we poured some dipperfuls of hot water over them, and shut the cover down; and the next morning, in our gingham gowns, we did up all the dish-washing for the day.

"Who folded all those clothes?" Why, we girls, of course. But you can't be told everything in one chapter.

CHAPTER VII.

SPRINKLES AND GUSTS.

RS. DUNIKIN used to bring them in, almost all of them, and leave them heaped up in the large round basket. Then there was the second-sized basket, into which they would all go comfortably when they were folded up.

One Monday night we went down as usual; some of us came in, — for we had been playing croquet until into the twilight, and the Haddens had just gone away, so we were later than usual at our laundry work. Leslie and Harry went round with Rosamond to the front door; Ruth slipped in at the back, and mother came down when she found that Rosamond had not been released. Barbara finished setting the tea-table, which she had a way of doing in a whiff, put on the sweet loaf upon the white trencher, and the dish of raspberry jam and the little silver-wire basket of crisp sugar-cakes, and then there was nothing but the tea, which stood ready for drawing in the small Japanese pot. Tea was nothing to get, ever.

" Mother, go back again ! You tired old darling, Ruth and I are going to do these ! " and Barbara plunged in among the " blossoms."

That was what we called the fresh, sweet-smelling white things. There are a great many pretty pieces of life, if you only know about them. Hay-making is one ; and rose-gathering is one ; and sprinkling and folding a great basket full of white clothes right out of the grass and the air and the sunshine is one.

Mother went off, — chiefly to see that Leslie and Harry were kept to tea, I believe. She knew how to compensate, in her lovely little underhand way, with Barbara.

Barbara pinned up her muslin sleeves to the shoulder, shook out a little ruffled short-skirt and put it on for an apron, took one end of the long white ironing-table that stood across the window, pushed the water-basin into the middle, and began with the shirts and the starched things. Ruth, opposite, was making the soft underclothing into little white rolls.

Barbara dampened and smoothed and stretched ; she almost ironed with her fingers, Mrs. Dunikin said. She patted and evened, laid collars and cuffs one above another with a sprinkle of drops, just from her finger-ends, between, and then gave a towel a nice equal shower with a corn-whisk that she used for the large things, and rolled them up in it, hard and fast, with a thump of her round pretty fist upon the middle before she laid it by. It was

a clever little process to watch; and her arms were white
in the twilight. Girls can't do all the possible pretty ma-
nœuvres in the German or out at croquet, if they only
once knew it. They do find it out in a one-sided sort of
way; and then they run to private theatricals. But the
real every-day scenes are just as nice, only they must have
their audiences in ones and twos; perhaps not always
any audience at all.

Of a sudden Ruth became aware of an audience of one.

Upon the balcony, leaning over the rail, looking right
down into the nearest kitchen window and over Barbara's
shoulder, stood Harry Goldthwaite. He shook his head at
Ruth, and she held her peace.

Barbara began to sing. She never sang to the piano, —
only about her work. She made up little snatches, piece-
meal, of various things, and put them to any sort of words.
This time it was to her own, — her poem.

> " I wrote some little books ;
> I said some little says ;
> I preached a little pre-e-each ;
> I lit a little blaze ;
> I made — things — pleasant — in one — little — place."

She ran down a most contented little trip, with repeats
and returns, in a G-octave, for the last line. Then she
rolled up a bundle of shirts in a square pillow-case, gave
it its accolade, and pressed it down into the basket.

"How do you suppose, Ruth, we shall manage the
town-meetings? Do you believe they will be as nice as
this? Where shall we get our little inspirations, after we
have come out of all our corners?"

"We won't do it," said Ruth, quietly, shaking out one

of mother's nightcaps, and speaking under the disadvantage of her private knowledge.

" I think they ought to let us vote just once," said Barbara ; " to say whether we ever would again. I believe we 're in danger of being put upon now, if we never were before."

" It is n't fair," said Ruth, with her eyes up out of the window at Harry, who made noiseless motion of clapping his hands. How could she tell what Barbara would say next, or how she would like it when she knew ?

" Of course it is n't," said Barbara, intent upon the gathers of a white cambric waist of Rosamond's. " I wonder, Ruth, if we shall have to read all those Pub. Doc.s that father gets. You see women will make awful hard work of it, if they once do go at it ; they are so used to doing every — little — thing " ; and she picked out the neck-edging, and smoothed the hem between the buttons.

" We shall have to take vows, and devote ourselves to it," Barbara went on, as if she were possessed. " There will have to be ' Sisters of Polity.' Not that I ever will. I don't feel a vocation. I 'd rather be a Polly-put-the-kettle-on all the days of my life."

" Mr. Goldthwaite ! " said Ruth.

" May I ? " asked Harry, as if he had just come, leaning down over the rail, and speaking to Barbara, who faced about with a jump.

She knew by his look ; he could not keep in the fun.

" ' *May* you ' ? When you have already ! "

" O no, I have n't ! I mean, come down ? Into the one-pleasant-little-place, and help ? "

" You don't know the way," Barbara said, stolidly, turning back again, and folding up the waist.

"Don't I? Which, — to come down, or to help?" and Harry flung himself over the rail, clasped one hand and wrist around a copper water-pipe that ran down there, reached the other to something above the window, — the mere pediment, I believe, — and swung his feet lightly to the sill beneath. Then he dropped himself and sat down, close by Barbara's elbow.

"You 'll get sprinkled," said she, flourishing the corn-whisk over a table-cloth.

"I dare say. Or patted, or punched, or something. I knew I took the risk of all that when I came down amongst it. But it looked nice. I could n't help it, and I don't care!"

Barbara was thinking of two things, — how long he had been there, and what in the world she had said besides what she remembered; and — how she should get off her rough-dried apron.

"Which do you want, — napkins or pillow-cases?" and he came round to the basket, and began to pull out.

"Napkins," says Barbara.

The napkins were underneath, and mixed up; while he stooped and fumbled, she had the ruffled petticoat off over her head. She gave it a shower in such a hurry, that as Harry came up with the napkins, he did get a drift of it in his face.

"That won't do," said Barbara, quite shocked, and tossing the whisk aside. "There are too many of us."

She began on the napkins, sprinkling with her fingers. Harry spread up a pile on his part, dipping also into the bowl. "I used to do it when I was a little boy," he said.

8

Ruth took the pillow-cases, and so they came to the last. They stretched the sheets across the table, and all three had a hand in smoothing and showering.

"Why, I wish it were n't all done," says Harry, turning over three clothes-pins in the bottom of the basket, while Barbara buttoned her sleeves. "Where does this go? What a nice place this is!" looking round the clean kitchen, growing shadowy in the evening light. "I think your house is full of nice places."

"Are you nearly ready, girls?" came in mother's voice from above.

"Yes, ma'am," Harry answered back, in an excessively cheery way. "We 're coming"; and up the stairs all three came together, greatly to Mrs. Holabird's astonishment.

"You never know where help is coming from when you 're trying to do your duty," said Barbara, in a highmoral way. "Prince Percinet, Mrs. Holabird."

"Miss Polly-put — " began Harry Goldthwaite, brimming up with a half-diffident mischief. But Barbara walked round to her place at the table with a very great dignity.

People think that young folks can only have properly arranged and elaborately provided good times; with Germania band pieces, and bouquets and ribbons for the German, and oysters and salmon-salad and sweatmeat-and-spun-sugar "chignons"; at least, commerce games and bewitching little prizes. Yet when lives just touch each other naturally, as it were, — dip into each other's little interests and doings, and take them as they are, what a multiplication-table of opportunities it opens up! You

may happen upon a good time any minute, then. Neigh-
borhoods used to go on in that simple fashion; life used
to be " co-operative."

Mother said something like that after Leslie and Harry
had gone away.

" Only you can't get them into it again," objected
Rosamond. "It's a case of Humpty Dumpty. The
world will go on."

" *One* world will," said Barbara. " But the world is
manifold. You can set up any kind of a monad you like,
and a world will shape itself round it. You 've just got
to live your own way, and everything that belongs to it
will be sure to join on. You 'll have a world before you
know it. I think myself that 's what the Ark means, and
Mount Ararat, and the Noachian — don't they call it ? —
new foundation. That 's the way they got up New England, anyhow."

" Barbara, what flights you take ! "

" Do I ? Well, we have to. The world lives up
nineteen flights now, you know, besides the old broken-
down and buried ones."

It was a few days after that, that the news came to
mother of Aunt Radford's illness, and she had to go
up to Oxenham. Father went with her, but he came
back the same night. Mother had made up her mind
to stay a week. And so we had to keep house without
her.

One afternoon Grandfather Holabird came down. I
don't know why, but if ever mother did happen to be out
of the way, it seemed as if he took the time to talk over
special affairs with father. Yet he thought everything of

" Mrs. Stephen," too, and he quite relied upon her judgment and influence. But I think old men do often feel as if they had got their sons back again, quite to themselves, when the Mrs. Stephens or the Mrs. Johns leave them alone for a little.

At any rate, Grandfather Holabird sat with father on the north piazza, out of the way of the strong south-wind; and he had out a big wallet, and a great many papers, and he stayed and stayed, from just after dinner-time till almost the middle of the afternoon, so that father did not go down to his office at all; and when old Mr. Holabird went home at last, he walked over with him. Just after they had gone Leslie Goldthwaite and Harry stopped, " for a minute only," they said; for the south-wind had brought up clouds, and there was rain threatening. That was how we all happened to be just as we were that night of the September gale; for it was the September gale of last year that was coming.

The wind had been queer, in gusts, all day; yet the weather had been soft and mild. We had opened windows for the pleasant air, and shut them again in a hurry when the papers blew about, and the pictures swung to and fro against the walls. Once that afternoon, somebody had left doors open through the brown room and the dining-room, where a window was thrown up, as we could have it there where the three were all on one side. Ruth was coming down stairs, and saw grandfather's papers give a whirl out of his lap and across the piazza floor upon the gravel. If she had not sprung so quickly and gathered them all up for him, some of them might have blown quite away, and led father a chase after them over the hill. After that,

old Mr. Holabird put them up in his wallet again, and when they had talked a few minutes more they went off together to the old house.

It was wonderful how that wind and rain did come up. The few minutes that Harry and Leslie stopped with us, and then the few more they took to consider whether it would do for Leslie to try to walk home, just settled it that nobody could stir until there should be some sort of lull or holding up.

Out of the far southerly hills came the blast, rending and crashing ; the first swirls of rain that flung themselves

against our windows seemed as if they might have rushed
ten miles, horizontally, before they got a chance to drop;
the trees bent down and sprang again, and lashed the air
to and fro; chips and leaves and fragments of all strange
sorts took the wonderful opportunity and went soaring
aloft and onward in a false, plebeian triumph.

The rain came harder, in great streams; but it all went
by in white, wavy drifts; it seemed to rain from south to
north across the country, — not to fall from heaven to
earth; we wondered if it *would* fall anywhere. It beat
against the house; that stood up in its way; it rained
straight in at the window-sills and under the doors; we ran
about the house with cloths and sponges to sop it up from
cushions and carpets.

"I say, Mrs. Housekeeper!" called out Stephen from
above, "look out for father's dressing-room! It's all
afloat, — hair-brushes out on voyages of discovery, and a
horrid little kelpie sculling round on a hat-box!"

Father's dressing-room was a windowed closet, in the
corner space beside the deep, old-fashioned chimney. It
had hooks and shelves in one end, and a round shaving-
stand and a chair in the other. We had to pull down all
his clothes and pile them upon chairs, and stop up the
window with an old blanket. A pane was cracked, and
the wind, although its force was slanted here, had blown
it in, and the fine driven spray was dashed across, diago-
nally, into the very farthest corner.

In the room a gentle cascade descended beside the
chimney, and a picture had to be taken down. Down
stairs the dining-room sofa, standing across a window, got
a little lake in the middle of it before we knew. The side

door blew open with a bang, and hats, coats, and shawls went scurrying from their pegs, through sitting-room and hall, like a flight of scared, living things. We were like a little garrison in a great fort, besieged at all points at once. We had to bolt doors, — latches were nothing, — and bar shutters. And when we could pause indoors, what a froth and whirl we had to gaze out at!

The grass, all along the fields, was white, prostrate; swept fiercely one way; every blade stretched out helpless upon its green face. The little pear-trees, heavy with fruit, lay prone in literal " windrows." The great ashes and walnuts twisted and writhed, and had their branches stripped upward of their leaves, as a child might draw a head of blossoming grass between his thumb and finger. The beautiful elms were in a wild agony; their graceful little bough-tips were all snapped off and whirled away upon the blast, leaving them in a ragged blight. A great silver poplar went over by the fence, carrying the posts and palings with it, and upturned a huge mass of roots and earth, that had silently cemented itself for half a century beneath the sward. Up and down, between Grandfather Holabird's home-field and ours, fallen locusts and wild cherry-trees made an abatis. Over and through all swept the smiting, powdery, seething storm of waters; the air was like a sea, tossing and foaming; we could only see through it by snatches, to cry out that this and that had happened. Down below us, the roof was lifted from a barn, and crumpled up in a heap half a furlong off, against some rocks; and the hay was flying in great locks through the air.

It began to grow dark. We put a bright, steady light

in the brown room, to shine through the south window, and show father that we were all right; directly after a lamp was set in Grandfather Holabird's north porch. This little telegraphy was all we could manage; we were as far apart as if the Atlantic were between us.

"Will they be frightened about you at home?" asked Ruth of Leslie.

"I think not. They will know we should go in somewhere, and that there would be no way of getting out again. People must be caught everywhere, just as it happens, to-night."

"It's just the jolliest turn-up!" cried Stephen, who had been in an ecstasy all the time. "Let's make molasses-candy, and sit up all night!"

Between eight and nine we had some tea. The wind had lulled a little from its hurricane force; the rain had stopped.

"It had all been blown to Canada, by this time," Harry Goldthwaite said. "That rain never stopped anywhere short, except at the walls and windows."

True enough, next morning, when we went out, the grass was actually dry.

It was nearly ten when Stephen went to the south window and put his hands up each side of his face against the glass, and cried out that there was a lantern coming over from grandfather's. Then we all went and looked.

It came slowly; once or twice it stopped; and once it moved down hill at right angles quite a long way. "That is where the trees are down," we said. But presently it took an unobstructed diagonal, and came steadily on to the long piazza steps, and up to the side door that opened upon the little passage to the dining-room.

We thought it was father, of course, and we all hurried to the door to let him in, and at the same time to make it nearly impossible that he should enter at all. But it was Grandfather Holabird's man, Robert.

"The old gentleman has been taken bad," he said. "Mr. Stephen wants to know if you're all comfortable, and he won't come till Mr. Holabird's better. I've got to go to the town for the doctor."

"On foot, Robert?"

"Sure. There's no other way. I take it there's many a good winter's firing of wood down across the road atwixt here and there. There ain't much knowing where you *can* get along."

"But what is it?"

"We mustn't keep him," urged Barbara.

"No, I ain't goin' to be kep'. 'T won't do. I donne what it is. It's a kind of a turn. He's comin' partly out of it; but it's bad. He had a kind of a warnin' once before. It's his head. They're afraid it's appalectic, or paralettic, or sunthin'."

Robert looked very sober. He quite passed by the wonder of the gale, that another time would have stirred him to most lively speech. Robert "thought a good deal," as he expressed it, of Grandfather Holabird.

Harry Goldthwaite came through the brown room with his hat in his hand. How he ever found it we could not tell.

"I'll go with him," he said. "You won't be afraid now, will you, Barbara? I'm *very* sorry about Mr. Holabird."

He shook hands with Barbara, — it chanced that she stood nearest, — bade us all good night, and went away. We turned back silently into the brown room.

We were all quite hushed from our late excitement. What strange things were happening to-night!

All in a moment something so solemn and important was put into our minds. An event that, — never talked about, and thought of as little, I suppose, as such a one ever was in any family like ours, — had yet always loomed vaguely afar, as what should come some time, and would bring changes when it came, was suddenly impending.

Grandfather might be going to die.

And yet what was there for us to do but to go quietly back into the brown room and sit down?

There was nothing to say even. There never is anything to say about the greatest things. People can only name the bare, grand, awful fact, and say, " It was tremendous," or " startling," or " magnificent," or " terrible," or " sad." How little we could really say about the gale, even now that it was over ! We could repeat that this and that tree were blown down, and such a barn or house unroofed; but we could not get the real wonder of it — the thing that moved us to try to talk it over — into any words.

" He seemed so well this afternoon," said Rosamond.

" I don't think he *was* quite well," said Ruth. " His hands trembled so when he was folding up his papers ; and he was very slow."

" O, men always are with their fingers. I don't think that was anything," said Barbara. " But I think he seemed rather nervous when he came over. And he would not sit in the house, though the wind was coming up then. He said he liked the air; and he and father got the shaker chairs up there by the front door; and he sat and pinched his knees together to make a lap to hold his papers; it was as much as he could manage; no wonder his hands trembled."

"I wonder what they were talking about," said Rosamond.

"I'm glad Uncle Stephen went home with him," said Ruth.

"I wonder if we shall have this house to live in if grandfather should die," said Stephen, suddenly. It could not have been his *first* thought; he had sat soberly silent a good while.

"O Stevie! *don't* let's think anything about that!" said Ruth; and nobody else answered at all.

We sent Stephen off to bed, and we girls sat round the fire, which we had made up in the great open fireplace, till twelve o'clock; then we all went up stairs, leaving the side door unfastened. Ruth brought some pillows and comfortables into Rosamond and Barbara's room, made up a couch for herself on the box-sofa, and gave her little white one to Leslie. We kept the door open between. We could see the light in grandfather's northwest chamber; and the lamp was still burning in the porch below. We could not possibly know anything; whether Robert had got back, and the doctor had come, — whether he was better or worse, — whether father would come home to-night. We could only guess.

"O Leslie, it is so good you are here!" we said.

There **was something eerie in** the night, in the wreck and confusion **of the** storm, **in** our loneliness without father and mother, and **in the** possible awfulness and change that **were so near,** — over there in Grandfather Holabird's **lighted room.**

CHAPTER VIII.

HALLOWEEN.

BREAKFAST was late the next morning. It had been nearly two o'clock when father had come home. He told us that grandfather was better; that it was what the doctor called a premonitory attack; that he might have another and more serious one any day, or that he might live on for years without a repetition. For the present he was to be kept as easy and quiet as possible, and gradually allowed to resume his old habits as his strength permitted.

Mother came back in a few days more; Aunt Radford also was better. The family fell into the old ways again, and it was as if no change had threatened. Father told mother, however, something of importance that grandfather had said to him that afternoon, before he was taken ill. He had been on the point of showing him something which he looked for among his papers, just before the wind whirled them out of his hands. He had almost said he would complete and give it to him at once; and then, when they were interrupted, he had just put everything up again, and they had walked over home together. Then there had been the excitement of the gale, and grandfather had insisted upon going to the barns himself to see that all was made properly fast, and had come back all out of breath, and had been taken with that ill turn in the midst of the storm.

The paper he was going to show to father was an unwitnessed deed of gift. He had thought of securing to us this home, by giving it in trust to father for his wife and children.

"I helped John into his New York business," he said, "by investing money in it that he has had the use of, at moderate interest, ever since; and Roderick and his wife have had their home with me. None of my boys ever paid me any *board*. I sha' n't make a will; the law gives things where they belong; there's nothing but this that wants evening; and so I've been thinking about it. What you do with your share of my other property when you get it is no concern of mine as I know of; but I should like to give you something in such a shape that it could n't go for old debts. I never undertook to shoulder any of *them;* what little I've done was done for you. I wrote out the paper myself; I never go to lawyers. I suppose it would stand clear enough for honest comprehension, — and Roderick and John are both honest, — if I left it as it is; but perhaps I 'd as well take it some day to Squire Hadden, and swear to it, and then hand it over to you. I 'll see about it."

That was what grandfather had said; mother told us all about it; there were no secret committees in our domestic congress; all was done in open house; we knew all the hopes and the perplexities, only they came round to us in due order of hearing. But father had not really seen the paper, after all; and after grandfather got well, he never mentioned it again all that winter. The wonder was that he had mentioned it at all.

"He forgets a good many things, since his sickness," father said, "unless something comes up to remind him. But there is the paper; he must come across that."

"He may change his mind," said mother, "even when he does recollect. We can be sure of nothing."

But we grew more fond than ever of the old, sunshiny house. In October Harry Goldthwaite went away again on a year's cruise.

Rosamond had a letter from Mrs. Van Alstyne, from New York. She folded it up after she had read it, and did not tell us anything about it. She answered it next day; and it was a month later when one night up stairs she began something she had to say about our winter shopping with, —

"If I had gone to New York — " and there she stopped, as if she had accidentally said what she did not intend.

"If you had gone to New York! Why! When?" cried Barbara. "What do you mean?"

"Nothing," Rosamond answered, in a vexed way. "Mrs. Van. Alstyne asked me, that is all. Of course I could n't."

"Of course you 're just a glorious old *noblesse oblige*-d!

Why did n't you say something? You might have gone perhaps. We could all have helped. I'd have lent you — that garnet and white silk!"

Rosamond would not say anything more, and she would scarcely be kissed.

After all, she had co-operated more than any of us. Rose was always the daughter who objected and then did. I have often thought that young man in Scripture ought to have been a woman. It is more a woman's way.

The maples were in their gold and vermilion now, and the round masses of the ash were shining brown; we filled the vases with their leaves, and pressed away more in all the big books we could confiscate, and hunted frosted ferns in the wood-edge, and had beautiful pine blazes morning and evening in the brown room, and began to think how pleasant, for many cosey things, the winter was going to be, out here at Westover.

"How nicely we could keep Halloween," said Ruth, "round this great open chimney! What a row of nuts we could burn!"

"So we will," said Rosamond. "We'll ask the girls. May n't we, mother?"

"To tea?"

"No. Only to the fun, — and some supper. We can have that all ready in the other room."

"They'll see the cooking-stove."

"They won't know it, when they do," said Barbara.

"We might have the table in the front room," suggested Ruth.

"The drawing-room!" cried Rosamond. "That would be a make-shift. Who ever heard of having supper there? No; we 'll have both rooms open, and a bright fire in each, and one up in mother's room for them to take off their things. And there 'll be the piano, and the stereoscope, and the games, in the parlor. We 'll begin in there, and out here we 'll have the fortune tricks and the nuts later; and then the supper, bravely and comfortably, in the dining-room, where it belongs. If they get frightened at anything, they can go home; I 'm going to new cover that screen, though, mother; And I 'll tell you what with, — that piece of goldy-brown damask up in the cedar-trunk. And I 'll put an arabesque of crimson braid around it for a border, and the room will be all goldy-brown and crimson then, and nobody will stop to think which is brocade and which is waterproof. They 'll be sitting on the waterproof, you know, and have the brocade to look at. It 's just old enough to seem as if it had always been standing round somewhere."

"It will be just the kind of party for us to have," said Barbara.

"They could n't have it up there, if they tried. It would be sure to be Marchbanksy."

Rosamond smiled contentedly. She was beginning to recognize her own special opportunities. She was quite conscious of her own tact in utilizing them.

But then came the intricate questions of who? and who not?

"Not everybody, of course," said Rose, "That would be a confusion. Just the neighbors, — right around here."

"That takes in the Hobarts, and leaves out Leslie Goldthwaite," said Ruth, quietly.

9

"O, Leslie will be at the Haddens', or here," replied Rosamond. "Grace Hobart is nice," she went on; "if only she would n't be 'real' nice!"

"That is just the word for her, though," said Ruth. "The Hobarts *are* real."

Rosamond's face gathered over. It was not easy to reconcile things. She liked them all, each in their way. If they would only all come, and like each other.

"What is it, Rose?" said Barbara, teasing. "Your brows are knit,— your nose is crocheted,— and your mouth is — tatted! I shall have to come and ravel you out."

"I 'm thinking; that is all."

"How to build the fence?"

"What fence?"

"That fence round the pond, — the old puzzle. There was once a pond, and four men came and built four little houses round it, — close to the water. Then four other men came and built four big houses, exactly behind the first ones. They wanted the pond all to themselves; but the little people were nearest to it; how could they build the fence, you know? They had to squirm it awfully! You see the plain, insignificant people are so apt to be nearest the good time!"

"I like to satisfy everybody."

"You won't, — with a squirm-fence!"

If it had not been for Ruth, we should have gone on just as innocently as possible, and invited them — March-bankses and all — to our Halloween frolic. But Ruth was such a little news-picker, with her music lessons! She had five scholars now; beside Lily and Reba, there were Elsie Hobart and little Frank Henace, and Pen Pennington, a girl of her own age, who had come all the way from Fort Vancouver, over the Pacific Railroad, to live here with her grandmother. Between the four houses, Ruth heard everything.

All Saints' Day fell on Monday; the Sunday made double hallowing, Barbara said; and Saturday was the "E'en." We did not mean to invite until Wednesday; on Tuesday Ruth came home and told us that Olivia and Adelaide Marchbanks were getting up a Halloween themselves, and that the Haddens were asked already; and that Lily and Reba were in transports because they were to be allowed to go.

"Did you say anything?" asked Rosamond.

"Yes. I suppose I ought not; but Elinor was in the room, and I spoke before I thought."

"What did you tell her?"

"I only said it was such a pity; that you meant to ask them all. And Elinor said it would be so nice here. If it were anybody else, we might try to arrange something."

But how could we meddle with the Marchbankses? With Olivia and Adelaide, of all the Marchbankses? We could not take it for granted that they meant to ask us. There was no such thing as suggesting a compromise. Rosamond looked high and splendid, and said not another word.

In the afternoon of Wednesday Adelaide and Maud Marchbanks rode by, homeward, on their beautiful little brown, long-tailed Morgans.

"They don't mean to," said Barbara. "If they did, they would have stopped."

"Perhaps they will send a note to-morrow," said Ruth.

"Do you think I am waiting, in hopes?" asked Rosamond, in her clearest, quietest tones.

Pretty soon she came in with her hat on.   "I am going over to invite the Hobarts," she said.

"That will settle it, whatever happens," said Barbara.

"Yes," said Rosamond; and she walked out.

The Hobarts were "ever so much obliged to us; and they would certainly come."   Mrs. Hobart lent Rosamond an old English book of "Holiday Sports and Observances," with ten pages of Halloween charms in it.

From the Hobarts' house she walked on into Z——, and asked Leslie Goldthwaite and Helen Josselyn, begging Mrs. Ingleside to come too, if she would; the doctor would call for them, of course, and should have his supper; but it was to be a girl-party in the early evening.

Leslie was not at home; Rosamond gave the message to her mother.   Then she met Lucilla Waters in the street.

"I was just thinking of you," she said.   She did not say, "coming to you," for truly, in her mind, she had not decided it.   But seeing her gentle, refined face, pale always with the life that had little frolic in it, she spoke right out to that, without deciding.

"We want you at our Halloween party on Saturday. Will you come?   You will have Helen and the Inglesides to come with, and perhaps Leslie."

Rosamond, even while delivering her message to Mrs. Goldthwaite for Leslie, had seen an unopened note lying upon the table, addressed to her in the sharp, tall hand of Olivia Marchbanks.

She stopped in at the Haddens, told them how sorry she had been to find they were promised ; asked if it were any use to go to the Hendees' ; and when Elinor said, " But you will be sure to be asked to the Marchbankses yourselves," replied, " It is a pity they should come together, but we had quite made up our minds to have this little frolic, and we have begun, too, you see."

Then she did go to the Hendees', although it was dark ; and Maria Hendee, who seldom went out to parties, promised to come. " They would divide," she said. " Fanny might go to Olivia's. Holiday-keeping was different from other invites. One might take liberties."

Now the Hendees were people who could take liberties, if anybody. Last of all, Rosamond went in and asked Pen Pennington.

It was Thursday, just at dusk, when Adelaide Marchbanks walked over, at last, and proffered her invitation.

" You had better all come to us," she said, graciously. " It is a pity to divide. We want the same people, of course, — the Hendees, and the Haddens, and Leslie." She hardly attempted to disguise that we ourselves were an afterthought.

Rosamond told her, very sweetly, that we were obliged, but that she was afraid it was quite too late ; we had asked others ; the Hobarts, and the Inglesides ; one or two whom Adelaide did not know, — Helen Josselyn, and Lucilla Waters ; the parties would not interfere much, after all.

Rosamond took up, as it were, a little sceptre of her own, from that moment.

Leslie Goldthwaite had been away for three days, stay-

ing with her friend, Mrs. Frank Scherman, in Boston.
She had found Olivia's note, of Monday evening, when
she returned; also, she heard of Rosamond's verbal invitation. Leslie was very bright about these things. She
saw in a moment how it had been. Her mother told her
what Rosamond had said of who were coming, — the Hobarts and Helen; the rest were not then asked."

Olivia did not like it very well, — that reply of Leslie's. She showed it to Jeannie Hadden; that was how
we came to know of it.

"Please forgive me," the note ran, "if I accept Rosamond's invitation for the very reason that might seem to
oblige me to decline it. I see you have two days' advan-
tage of her, and she will no doubt lose some of the girls by
that. I really *heard* hers first. I wish very much it
were possible to have both pleasures."

That was being terribly true and independent with
West Z——. "But Leslie Goldthwaite," Barbara said,
"always was as brave as a little bumble-bee!"

How it had come over Rosamond, though, we could
not quite understand. It was not pique, or rivalry;
there was no excitement about it; it seemed to be a pure,
spirited dignity of her own, which she all at once, quietly
and of course, asserted.

Mother said something about it to her Saturday morning, when she was beating up Italian cream, and Rosamond was cutting chicken for the salad. The cakes and
the jellies had been made the day before.

"You have done this, Rosamond, in a very right and
neighborly way, but it is n't exactly your old way. How
came you not to mind?"

Rosamond did not discuss the matter; she only smiled and said, " I think, mother, I 'm growing very proud and self-sufficient, since we 've had real, *through-and-through* ways of our own."

It was the difference between " somewhere " and " betwixt and between."

Miss Elizabeth Pennington came in while we were putting candles in the bronze branches, and Ruth was laying an artistic fire in the wide chimney. Ruth could make a picture with her crossed and balanced sticks, sloping the firm-built pile backward to the two great, solid logs behind, — a picture which it only needed the touch of flame to finish and perfect. Then the dazzling fire-wreaths curled and clasped through and about it all, filling the spaces with a rushing splendor, and reaching up their vivid spires above its compact body to an outline of complete live beauty. Ruth's fires satisfied you to look at: and they never tumbled down.

She rose up with a little brown, crooked stick in one hand, to speak to Miss Pennington.

" Don't mind me," said the lady. " Go on, please, ' biggin' your castle.' That will be a pretty sight to see, when it lights up."

Ruth liked crooked sticks; they held fast by each other, and they made pretty curves and openings. So she went on, laying them deftly.

" I should like to be here to-night," said Miss Elizabeth, still looking at the fire-pile. " Would you let an old maid in ? "

" Miss Pennington ! Would you come ? "

" I took it in my head to want to. That was why

I came over. **Are** you going to play snap-dragon? **I**
wondered if you had thought of that."

" We don't know about **it,**" said **Ruth.** " Anything,
that is, except the name."

" That is just what **I** thought possible. **Nobody knows
those old games nowadays.** May I come and bring **a** great
dragon-bowl with **me,** and superintend that part? Mother
got her fate **out of a** snap-dragon, and we have the identi-
cal bowl. We always used to bring it out at Christmas,
when we were all at home."

" **O** Miss Pennington! How perfectly lovely! **How**
good you are ! "

" Well, I 'm glad you take **it so.** **I** was afraid it was
terribly meddlesome. But the fancy — or the memory —
seized me."

How wonderfully **our Halloween party was** turning
out!

And the turning-out is almost the best part of anything;
the time when things are getting together, in the beautiful prosperous way they will take, now and then, even in
this vexed world.

There was our lovely **little supper-table all** ready.
People who have servants enough, high-trained, to do
these **things while** they are entertaining in the drawing-
room, don't have half the pleasure, after all, that we do,
in setting **out** hours beforehand, and putting the **last**
touches and taking the final satisfaction before we go to
dress.

The cake, with the ring in it, was in the middle ; **for
we had** put together all the fateful and pretty customs we
could think of, **from** whatever holiday ; there were moth-

er's Italian creams, and amber and garnet wine jellies; there were sponge and lady-cake, and the little macaroons and cocoas that Barbara had the secret of; and the salad, of spring chickens and our own splendid celery, was ready in the cold room, with its bowl of delicious dressing to be poured over it at the last; and the scalloped oysters were in the pantry; Ruth was to put them into the oven again when the time came, and mother would pin the white napkins around the dishes, and set them on; and nobody was to worry or get tired with having the whole to think of; and yet the whole would be done, to the very lighting of the candles, which Stephen had spoken for, by this beautiful, organized co-operation of ours. Truly it is a charming thing, — all to itself, in a family!

To be sure, we had coffee and bread and butter and cold ham for dinner that day; and we took our tea " standed round," as Barbara said; and the dishes were put away in the covered sink; we knew where we could shirk righteously and in good order, when we could not accomplish everything; but there was neither huddle nor hurry; we were as quiet and comfortable as we could be. Even Rosamond was satisfied with the very manner; to be composed is always to be elegant. Anybody might have come in and lunched with us; anybody might have shared that easy, chatty cup of tea.

The front parlor did not amount to much, after all, pleasant and pretty as it was for the first receiving; we were all too eager for the real business of the evening. It was bright and warm with the wood-fire and the lights; and the white curtains, nearly filling up three of its walls, made it very festal-looking. There was the open piano, and Ruth played a little ; **there** was the stereoscope, and some of the girls looked **over the new** views of Catskill and the Hudson that **Dakie** Thayne **had** given us ; there was the table with cards, and **we** played **one** game of Old Maid, in which **the** Old Maid **got** lost mysteriously into **the drawer,** and everybody was married ; **and** then Miss **Pennington** appeared at the door, with her **man-ser-**vant **behind her, and** there was **an** end. She **took the** big **bowl, pinned over with** a great damask napkin, out **of the man's hands, and went** off privately with Barbara into **the** dining-room.

"**This is the** Snap," she **said,** unfastening the cover, and **producing** from within **a** paper parcel. " And that," holding **up** a little white bottle, **" is the** Dragon." And **Barbara** set all away **in the** dresser until after supper. **Then** we got together, without further ceremony, in the brown room.

We hung wedding-rings — we had mother's, and Miss Elizabeth **had** brought over Madam Pennington's — by hairs, **and** held them inside tumblers ; and they vibrated with our quickening pulses, and swung and **swung, until** they **rung out fairy chimes of** destiny against **the sides.** We **floated needles in a great basin of** water, **and** gave **them names, and watched them turn** and swim and draw **together, — some point** to point, **some** heads and points, **some** joined cosily side to side, while some drifted **to** the margin and clung there all alone, and some got tears in their eyes, or an interfering jostle, and went down. We melted lead and poured it into water ; and it took strange shapes ; of spears and masts and stars ; and some all **went** to money ; and one was a queer little bottle and

pills, and one was pencils and artists' tubes, and — really
— a little palette with a hole in it.

And then came the chestnut-roasting, before the bright
red coals. Each girl put down a pair; and I dare say
most of them put down some little secret, girlish thought
with it. The ripest nuts burned steadiest and surest, of
course; but how could we tell these until we tried?
Some little crack, or unseen worm-hole, would keep one
still, while its companion would pop off, away from it;
some would take flight together, and land in like manner,
without ever parting company; these were to go some
long way off; some never moved from where they began,
but burned up, stupidly and peaceably, side by side.

Some snapped into the fire.   Some went off into corners.
Some glowed beautiful, and some burned black, and some
got covered up with ashes.

Barbara's pair were ominously still for a time, when
all at once the larger gave a sort of unwilling lurch, without popping, and rolled off a little way, right in toward the
blaze.

" Gone to a warmer climate," whispered Leslie, like a
tease.   And then crack ! the warmer climate, or something else, sent him back again, with a real bound, just as
Barbara's gave a gentle little snap, and they both dropped
quietly down against the fender together.

" What made that jump back, I wonder ? " said Pen
Pennington.

" O, it was n't more than half cracked when it went
away," said Stephen, looking on.

Who would be bold enough to try the looking-glass ?
To go out alone with it into the dark field, walking backward, saying the rhyme to the stars which if there had
been a moon ought by right to have been said to her : —

> " Round and round, O stars so fair !
> Ye travel, and search out everywhere.
> I pray you, sweet stars, now show to me,
> This night, who my future husband shall be ! "

Somehow, we put it upon Leslie.   She was the oldest ;
we made that the reason.

" I would n't do it for anything ! " said Sarah Hobart.
" I heard of a girl who tried it once, and saw a shroud ! "

But Leslie was full of fun that evening, and ready to
do anything.   She took the little mirror that Ruth brought
her from up stairs, put on a shawl, and we all went to the
front door with her, to see her off.

"Round the piazza, and down the bank," said Barbara, "and backward all the way."

So Leslie backed out at the door, and we shut it upon her. The instant after, we heard a great laugh. Off the piazza, she had stepped backward, directly against two gentlemen coming in.

Doctor Ingleside was one, coming to get his supper; the other was a friend of his, just arrived in Z——. "Doctor John Hautayne," he said, introducing him by his full name.

We knew why. He was proud of it. Doctor John Hautayne was the army surgeon who had been with him in the Wilderness, and had ridden a stray horse across a battle-field, in his shirt-sleeves, right in front of a Rebel battery, to get to some wounded on the other side. And the Rebel gunners, holding their halyards, stood still and shouted.

It put an end to the tricks, except the snap-dragon.

We had not thought how late it was; but mother and Ruth had remembered the oysters.

Doctor John Hautayne took Leslie out to supper. We saw him look at her with a funny, twinkling curiosity, as he stood there with her in the full light; and we all thought we had never seen Leslie look prettier in all her life.

After supper, Miss Pennington lighted up her Dragon, and threw in her snaps. A very little brandy, and a bowl full of blaze.

Maria Hendee "snapped" first, and got a preserved date.

"Ancient and honorable," said Miss Pennington, laughing.

Then Pen Pennington tried, and got nothing.

"You thought of your own **fingers**," said her aunt.

"A fig for **my fortune !**" cried Barbara, holding up her trophy.

"It came from the Mediterranean," said **Mrs.** Ingleside, over her shoulder into her ear; and the ear burned.

Ruth **got a sugared** almond.

"Only a *kernel*," said the merry doctor's wife, **again.**

The doctor himself tried, and seized a slip **of** candied flag.

"**Warm-hearted and useful, that is all**," said Mrs. Ingleside.

"And tolerably **pungent**," said **the doctor.**

Doctor Hautayne drew forth — angelica.

Most of them **were too** timid **or** irresolute to grasp anything.

"That's the analogy," **said** Miss Pennington. "One must take the risk of getting scorched. It is 'the woman who dares,' after all."

It **was** great **fun,** though.

Mother **cut the cake.** That **was** the **last sport of the** evening.

If I should tell you who got the ring, you would think **it really meant something. And the** year is not out yet, you see.

But there was no doubt **of one** thing, — that our Halloween at **Westover was a** famous little party.

"**How do** you all feel about it ?" asked Barbara, sitting **down on** the hearth in the brown room, before the embers, **and** throwing the nuts she had picked up about the carpet **into the coals.**

We had carried the supper-dishes away into the out-room, and set them on a great spare table that we kept there. "The room is as good as the girl," said Barbara. It *is* a comfort to put by things, with a clear conscience, to a more rested time. We should let them be over the Sunday; Monday morning would be all china and soap-suds; then there would be a nice, freshly arrayed dresser, from top to bottom, and we should have had both a party and a piece of fall cleaning.

"How do you feel about it?"

"I feel as if we had had a real *own* party, ourselves," said Ruth; "not as if 'the girls' had come and had a party here. There was n't anybody to *show us how!*"

"Except Miss Pennington. And was n't it bewitchi-nating of her to come? Nobody can say now — "

"What do you say it for, then?" interrupted Rosa-mond. "It was very nice of Miss Pennington, and kind, considering it was a young party. Otherwise, why should n't she?"

CHAPTER IX.

WINTER NIGHTS AND WINTER DAYS.

"THAT was a nice party," said Miss Pennington, walking home with Leslie and Doctor John Hautayne, behind the Inglesides. "What made it so nice?"

"You, very much," said Leslie, straightforwardly.

"I did n't begin it," said Miss Elizabeth. "No; that was n't it. It was a step out, somehow. Out of the treadmill. I got tired of parties long ago, before I was old. They were all alike. The only difference was that in one house the staircase went up on the right side of the hall, and in another on the left, — now and then, perhaps, at the back; and when you came down again, the lady near the drawing-room door might be Mrs. Hendee one night and Mrs. Marchbanks another; but after that it was all the same. And O, how I did get to hate ice-cream!"

"This was a party of 'nexts,'" said Leslie, "instead of a selfsame."

"What a good time Miss Waters had — quietly! You could see it in her face. A pretty face!" Miss Elizabeth spoke in a lower tone, for Lucilla was just before the Inglesides, with Helen and Pen Pennington. "She works too hard, though. I wish she came out more."

"The 'nexts' have to get tired of books and mending-baskets, while the firsts are getting tired of ice-creams," replied Leslie. "Dear Miss Pennington, there are ever so many nexts, and people don't think anything about it!"

"So there are," said Miss Elizabeth, quietly. "People are very stupid. They don't know what will freshen themselves up. They think the trouble is with the confectionery, and so they try macaroon and pistachio instead of lemon and vanilla. Fresh people are better than fresh flavors. But I think we had everything fresh to-night. What a beautiful old home-y house it is!"

"And what a home-y family!" said Doctor John Hautayne.

"We have an old home-y house," said Miss Pennington, suddenly, "with landscape-papered walls and cosey, deep windows and big chimneys. And we don't half use it. Doctor Hautayne, I mean to have a party! Will you stay and come to it?"

"Any time within my two months' leave," replied Doctor Hautayne, "and with very great pleasure."

"So she will have it before very long," said Leslie, telling us about the talk the next day.

It! Well, when Miss Pennington took up a thing she

10

did take it up! That **does not come** in here, though, —
any **more of it.**

The Penningtons **are very** proud people. They have
not a very great **deal of** money, like the Haddens, and
they **are** not **foremost in** everything like **the** Marchbankses; **somehow they do** not seem to care to take **the**
trouble for **that; but they are so** *established;* it **is a fam-**
ily like **an old** tree, that is past its green branching **time,
and makes little** spread or summer show, but whose roots
reach out **away** underneath, and grasp more ground than
all the rest **put** together.

They live in an old **house that is just like** them. **It
has not a** new-fashioned **thing about it.** The walls are
square, plain brick, painted **gray; and** there **is a** low,
broad porch in front, **and** then terraces, flagged with
gray stone and bordered **with** flower-beds at each side
and below. They have peacocks and guinea-hens, and
more roses and lilies and larkspurs and foxgloves and nar-
cissus than flowers of any newer sort; and there are great
bushes of box **and** southernwood, that smell sweet as **you**
go **by.**

Old General Pennington **had been in the army all his**
life. **He was a captain at Lundy's Lane, and got a** wound
there which **gave him a** stiff **elbow ever after;** and his
oldest son **was** killed **in Mexico, just** after he had been
brevetted Major. **There is a** Major Pennington now, —
the younger brother, — out at Fort Vancouver; and he
is Pen's father. When her mother died, away out there,
he had to send her home. The Penningtons are just as
proud as the stars and stripes themselves; and their glory
is off the selfsame piece.

They made very much of Dakie Thayne when he was here, in their quiet, retired way; and they had always been polite and cordial to the Inglesides.

One morning, a little while after our party, mother was making an apple-pudding for dinner, when Madam Pennington and Miss Elizabeth drove round to the door.

Ruth was out at her lessons; Barbara was busy helping Mrs. Holabird. Rosamond went to the door, and let them into the brown room.

"Mother will be sorry to keep you waiting, but she will come directly. She is just in the middle of an apple-pudding."

Rosamond said it with as much simple grace of pride as if she had had to say, " Mother is busy at her modelling, and cannot leave her clay till she has damped and covered it." Her nice perception went to the very farthermost; it discerned the real best to be made of things, the best that was *ready* made, and put that forth.

" And I know," said Madam Pennington, " that an apple-pudding must not be left in the middle. I wonder if she would let an old woman who has lived in barracks come to her where she is?"

Rosamond's tact was superlative. She did not say, " I will go and see "; she got right up and said, " I am sure she will; please come this way," and opened the door, with a sublime confidence, full and without warning, upon the scene of operations.

" O, how nice!" said Miss Elizabeth; and Madam Pennington walked forward into the sunshine, holding her hand out to Mrs. Holabird, and smiling all the way from her smooth old forehead down to the " seventh beauty " of her dimple-cleft and placid chin.

" Why, this is really coming to see people ! " she said.

Mrs. Holabird's white hand did not even want dusting; she just laid down the bright little chopper with which she was reducing her flour and butter to a golden powder, and took Madam Pennington's nicely gloved fingers into her own, without a breath of apology. Apology ! It was very meek of her not to look at all set up.

Barbara rose from her chair with a red ringlet of apple-paring hanging down against her white apron, and seated herself again at her work when the visitors had taken the two opposite corners of the deep, cushioned sofa.

The red cloth was folded back across the end of the dining-table, and at the other end were mother's white board and rolling-pin, the pudding-cloth wrung into a twist out of the scald, and waiting upon a plate, and a pitcher of cold water with ice tinkling against its sides. Mother sat with the deal bowl in her lap, turning and mincing with the few last strokes the light, delicate dust of the pastry. The sunshine — work and sunshine always go so blessedly together — poured in, and filled the room up with life and glory.

" Why, this is the pleasantest room in all your house ! " said Miss Elizabeth.

" That is just what Ruth said it would be when we turned it into a kitchen," said Barbara.

" You don't mean that this is really your kitchen ! "

" I don't think we are quite sure what it is," replied Barbara, laughing. " We either dine in our kitchen or kitch in our dining-room ; and I don't believe we have found out yet which it is ! "

" You are wonderful people ! "

" You ought to have belonged to the army, and lived in quarters," said Mrs. Pennington. "Only you would have made your rooms so bewitching you would have been always getting turned out."

" Turned out ? "

" Yes ; by the ranking family. That is the way they do. The major turns out the captain, and the colonel the major. There 's no rest for the sole of your foot till you 're a general."

Mrs. Holabird set her bowl on the table, and poured in the ice-water. Then the golden dust, turned and cut lightly by the chopper, gathered into a tender, mellow mass, and she lifted it out upon the board. She shook out the scalded cloth, spread it upon the emptied bowl, sprinkled it snowy-thick with flour, rolled out the crust with a free quick movement, and laid it on, into the curve of the basin. Barbara brought the apples, cut up in white fresh slices, and slid them into the round. Mrs. Holabird folded over the edges, gathered up the linen cloth in her hands, tied it tightly with a string, and Barbara disappeared with it behind the damask screen, where a puff of steam went up in a minute that told the pudding was in. Then Mrs. Holabird went into the pantry-closet and washed her hands, that never really came to need more than a finger-bowl could do for them, and Barbara carried after her the board and its etceteras, and the red cloth was drawn on again, and there was nothing but a low, comfortable bubble in the chimney-corner to tell of housewifery or dinner.

" I wish it had lasted longer," said Miss Elizabeth. "I am afraid I shall feel like company again now."

" I am ashamed to tell you what I came for," said Madam Pennington. " It was to ask about a girl. Can I do anything with Winny Lafferty ? "

" I wish you could," said Mrs. Holabird, benevolently.

" She needs doing with," said Barbara.

" Your having her would be different from our doing so," said Mrs. Holabird. " I often think that one of the tangles in the girl-question is the mistake of taking the rawest specimens into families that keep but one. With your Lucy, it might be the very making of Winny to go to you."

" The ' next ' for her, as Ruth would say," said Barbara.

" Yes. The least little thing that comes next is better than a world full of wisdom away off beyond. There is too much in ' general housework ' for one ignorant, inexperienced brain to take in. " What should we think of a government that gave out its ' general field-work ' so ? "

" There won't be any Lucys long," said Madam Pennington, with a sigh. " What are homes coming to ? "

" Back to *homes*, I hope, from *houses* divided against themselves into parlors and kitchens," said mother, earnestly. " If I should tell you all I think about it, you would say it was visionary, I am afraid. But I believe we have got to go back to first principles ; and then the Lucys will grow again."

" Modern establishments are not homes truly," said Madam Pennington.

" We shall call them by their names, as the French do, if we go on," said mother, — " hotels."

" And how are we to stop, or help it ? The enemy has got possession. Irishocracy is a despotism in the land."

"Only," said mother, in her sweetest, most heartfelt way, " by learning how true it is that one must be chief to really serve ; that it takes the highest to do perfect ministering; that the brightest grace and the most beautiful culture must come to bear upon this little, every-day living, which is all that the world works for after all. The whole heaven is made that just the daily bread for human souls may come down out of it. Only the Lord God can pour this room full of little waves of sunshine, and make a still, sweet morning in the earth."

Mother and Madam Pennington looked at each other with soulful eyes.

" ' We girls,' " began mother again, smiling, — " for that is the way the children count me in, — said to each other, when we first tried this new plan, that we would make an art-kitchen. We meant we would have things nice and pretty for our common work ; but there is something behind that, — the something that 'makes the meanest task divine,' — the spiritual correspondence of it. When we are educated up to that I think life and society will be somewhat different. I think we shall not always stop short at the drawing-room, and pretend at each other on the surface of things. I think the time may come when young girls and single women will be as willing, and think it as honorable, to go into homes which they need, and which need them, and give the best that they have grown to into the commonwealth of them, as they are willing now to educate and try for public places. And it will seem to them as great and beautiful a thing to do. They won't be buried, either. When they take the work up, and glorify it, it will glorify them. We don't know yet **what** households might be, **if now** we have got **the wheels so** perfected, we would **put** the living spirit into the wheels. They are **the motive power ;** homes are the primary meetings. **They would be** little kingdoms, of great might **!** I *wish* women would be content with their mainspring **work, and not want to go out and point** the time upon **the dial ! "**

Mother **never would** have made so long a speech, **but** that beautiful old Mrs. Pennington was answering her back **all the time out of** her eyes. **There** was such a magnet-**ism between** them **for** the moment, that she scarcely knew **she was** saying it **all.** The color came up in their cheeks, **and** they **were** young and splendid, **both** of them. **We** thought it **was as good a Woman's** Convention as if there **had** been **two** thousand **of them** instead **of two.** And when some of the things **out** of **the** closets get up on the **house-tops,** maybe it will prove **so.**

Madam Pennington leaned over and kissed mother when she took her hand at going away. And then Miss Elizabeth spoke **out** suddenly, —

" I have not done my errand **yet,** Mrs. Holabird. **Mother has taken up all the** time. **I want to have** some *nexts.* **Your girls know what I** mean ; **and I** want them **to take hold and help. They are going** to be ' next Thursdays,' **and to begin this** very coming Thursday of **all.** I shall give primary invitations only, — and my primaries are to find secondaries. **No** household is to rep-resent merely itself ; one or two, or more, from one fam-ily **are** to bring always one or two, or more, from some-where else. **I am** going **to** try if one little bit **of social life cannot be exogenous ;** and if it can, **what the** branching-out will come to. I think we want sapwood as well as heartwood to keep us green. If anybody does n't quite understand, refer to 'How Plants Grow — Gray.'"

She went off, leaving us that to think of.

Two days after she looked in again, and said more.

"Besides that, every primary or season invitation imposes a condition. Each member is to provide one practical answer to 'What next?' 'Next Thursday' is always to be in charge of somebody. You may do what you like, or can, with it. I'll manage the first myself. After that I wash my hands."

Out of it grew fourteen incomparable Thursday evenings. Pretty much all we can do about them is to tell that they were; we should want fourteen new numbers to write their full history. It was like Mr. Hale's lovely "Ten Times One is Ten." They all came from that one blessed little Halloween party of ours. It means something that there *is* such a thing as the multiplication-table; does n't it? You can't help yourself if you start a unit, good or bad. The Garden of Eden, and the Ark, and the Loaves and Fishes, and the Hundred and Forty-four Thousand sealed in their foreheads, tell of it, all through the Bible, from first to last. "Multiply!" was the very next, inevitable commandment, after the "Let there be!"

It was such a thing as had never rolled up, or branched out, though, in Westover before. The Marchbankses did not know what to make of it. People got in who had never belonged. There they were, though, in the stately old Pennington house, that was never thrown open for nothing; and when they were once there you really could not

tell the difference; unless, indeed, it were that the old,
middle wood was the deadest, just as it is in the trees;
and that the life was in the new sap and the green rind.

Lucilla Waters invented charades; and Helen Josselyn
acted them, as charades had never been acted on West
Hill until now. When it came to the Hobarts' "Next
Thursday" they gave us "Dissolving Views," — every
successive queer fashion that had come up resplendent
and gone down grotesque in these last thirty years. Mrs.
Hobart had no end of old relics, — bandbaskets packed
full of venerable bonnets, that in their close gradation of
change seemed like one individual Indur passing through
a metempsychosis of millinery; nests of old hats that were
odder than the bonnets; swallow-tailed coats; broad-
skirted blue ones with brass buttons; baby waists and
basquines; leg-of-mutton sleeves, balloons, and military;
collars inch-wide and collars ell-wide with ruffles *rayon-
nantes*; gathers and gores, tunnel-skirts, and barrel-skirts
and paniers. She made monstrous paper dickeys, and
high black stocks, and great bundling neckcloths; the
very pocket-handkerchiefs were as ridiculous as anything,
from the waiter-napkin size of good stout cambric to a
quarter-dollar bit of a middle with a cataract of "chan-
delier" lace about it. She could tell everybody how to do
their hair, from "flat curls" and "scallops" down or up
to frizzes and chignons; and after we had all filed in
slowly, one by one, and filled up the room, I don't think
there ever could have been a funnier evening!

We had musical nights, and readings. We had a
"Mutual Friend" Thursday; that was Mrs. Ingleside's.
Rosamond was the Boofer Lady; Barbara was Lavvy the

Irrepressible; and Miss Pennington herself was Mrs. Wilfer; Mr. and Mrs. Hobart were the Boffins; and Doctor Ingleside, with a wooden leg strapped on, dropped into poetry in the light of a friend; Maria Hendee came in twisting up her back hair, as Pleasant Riderhood, — Maria Hendee's back hair was splendid; Leslie looked very sweet and quiet as Lizzie Hexam, and she brought with her for her secondary that night the very, real little doll's dressmaker herself, — Maddy Freeman, who has carved brackets, and painted lovely book-racks and easels and vases and portfolios for almost everybody's parlors, and yet never gets into them herself.

Leslie would not have asked her to be Jennie Wren,

because she really has a lame foot; but when they told
her about it, she said right off, " O, how I wish I could
be that ! "   She has not only the lame foot, but the wonderful " golden bower " of sunshiny hair too ; and she
knows the doll's dressmaker by heart; she says she ex-
pects to find her some time, if ever she goes to England
— or to heaven.   Truly she was up to the " tricks and
the manners " of the occasion ; nobody entered into it
with more self-abandonment than she ; she was so com-
pletely Jennie Wren that no one — at the moment —
thought of her in any other character, or remembered
their rules of behaving according to the square of the distance.   She " took patterns " of Mrs. Lewis Marchbanks's trimmings to her very face ; she reached up behind Mrs. Linceford, and measured the festoon of her
panier.   There was no reason why she should be afraid
or abashed ; Maddy Freeman is a little lady, only she is
poor, and a genius.   She stepped right *out* of Dickens's
story, not *into* it, as the rest of us did ; neither did she
even seem to step consciously into the grand Pennington
house ; all she did as to that was to go " up here," or
" over there," and " be dead," as fresh, new-world de-
lights attracted her.   Lizzie Hexam went too ; they belonged together ; and T'other Governor would insist on
following after them, and being comfortably dead also,
though Society was behind him, and the Veneerings and
the Podsnaps looking on.   Mrs. Ingleside did not provide
any Podsnaps or Veneerings ; she said they would be
there.

    Now Eugene Wrayburn was Doctor John Hautayne;
for this was only our fourth evening.   Nobody had any-

thing to say about parts, except the person whose "next" it was; people had simply to take what they were helped to.

We began to be a little suspicious of **Doctor** Hautayne; to wonder about his " what next." Leslie behaved as if she had always **known** him; I believe it seemed **to** her as if she always had ; some lives meet in a way like that.

It did not end with parties, Miss Pennington's exogenous experiment. She did not mean it should. A great deal that was glad and comfortable came of it to many persons. Miss Elizabeth asked Maddy **Freeman** to " come up and be dead" whenever she felt like it; she goes there every week now, to copy pictures, and get rare little bits for her designs out of the Penningtons' great portfolios of engravings and drawings of ancient ornamentations ; and half the time they keep her to luncheon or to tea. Lucilla **Waters** knows them now as well as we do; and she is taking German lessons with **Pen Pennington.**

It really seems as if the " nexts" would grow on so that at last it would only be our old " set" that would be in any danger of getting left out. " Society is like a coral island after all," says Leslie Goldthwaite. " It isn't a rock of the Old Silurian."

It was a memorable winter to us in many ways, — that last winter of the nineteenth century's seventh decade.

One day — everything has to be one day, and all in a minute, when it does come, however many days lead up to it — Doctor Ingleside came in and told us the news. He had been up to see Grandfather Holabird; grandfather was not quite well.

They told him at home, the doctor said, not to stop any-

where; he knew what they meant by that, but he did n't
care; it was as much his news as anybody's, and why
should he be kept down to pills and plasters?

Leslie was going to marry Doctor John Hautayne.

Well! It was splendid news, and we had somehow
expected it. And yet — "only think!" That was all
we could say; that is a true thing people do say to each
other, in the face of a great, beautiful fact. Take it in;
shut your door upon it; and — think! It is something
that belongs to heart and soul.

We counted up; it was only seven weeks.

"As if that were the whole of it!" said Doctor Ingleside. "As if the Lord did n't know! As if they had n't
been living on, to just this meeting-place! She knows
his life, and the sort of it, though she has never been in
it with him before; that is, we'll concede that, for the
sake of argument, though I'm not so sure about it; and
he has come right here into hers. They are fair, open,
pleasant ways, both of them; and here, from the joining,
they can both look back and take in, each the other's;
and beyond they just run into one, you see, as foreor-
dained, and there's no other way for them to go."

Nobody knew it but ourselves that next night, —
Thursday. Doctor Hautayne read beautiful things from
the Brownings at Miss Pennington's that evening; it
was his turn to provide; but for us, — we looked into
new depths in Leslie's serene, clear, woman eyes, and
felt the intenser something in his face and voice, and the
wonder was that everybody could not see how quite
another thing than any merely written poetry was really
"next" that night for Leslie and for John Hautayne.

That was in December; it was the first of March when Grandfather Holabird died.

At about Christmas-time mother had taken a bad cold. We could not let her get up in the mornings to help before breakfast; the winter work was growing hard; there were two or three fires to manage besides the furnace, which father attended to; and although our "chore-man" came and split up kindlings and filled the wood-boxes, yet we were all pretty well tired out, sometimes, just with keeping warm. We began to begin to say things to each other which nobody actually finished. "If mother does n't get better," and "If this cold weather keeps on," and "*Are* we going to co-operate ourselves to death, do you think?" from Barbara, at last.

Nobody said, "We shall have to get a girl again." Nobody wanted to do that; and everybody had a secret feeling of Aunt Roderick, and her prophecy that we "should n't hold out long." But we were crippled and reduced; Ruth had as much as ever she could do, with the short days and her music.

"I begin to believe it was easy enough for Grant to say 'all *summer*,'" said Barbara; "but *this* is Valley Forge." The kitchen fire would n't burn, and the thermometer was down to 3° above. Mother was worrying up stairs, we knew, because we would not let her come down until it was warm and her coffee was ready.

That very afternoon Stephen came in from school with a word for the hour.

"The Stilkings are going to move right off to New Jersey," said he. "Jim Stilking told me so. The doctor says his father can't stay here."

"Arctura Fish won't go," said Rosamond, instantly.

"Arctura Fish is as neat as a pin, and as smart as a steel trap," said Barbara, regardless of elegance; "and — since nobody else will ever dare to give in — I believe Arctura Fish is the very next thing, now, for us!"

"It is n't giving in; it is going on," said Mrs. Holabird.

It certainly was not going back.

"We have got through ploughing-time, and now comes seed-time, and then harvest," said Barbara. "We shall raise, upon a bit of renovated earth, the first millennial specimen, — see if we don't! — of what was supposed to be an extinct flora, — the *Domestica antediluviana.*"

Arctura Fish came to us.

If you once get a new dress, or a new dictionary, or a new convenience of any kind, did you never notice that you immediately have occasions which prove that you could n't have lived another minute without it? We could not have spared Arctura a single day, after that, all winter. Mother gave up, and was ill for a fortnight. Stephen twisted his foot skating, and was laid up with a sprained ankle.

And then, in February, grandfather was taken with that last fatal attack, and some of us had to be with Aunt Roderick nearly all the time during the three weeks that he lived.

When they came to look through the papers there was no will found, of any kind; neither was that deed of gift.

Aunt Trixie was the only one out of the family who knew anything about it. She had been the "family bosom," Barbara said, ever since she cuddled us up in our baby blankets, and told us "this little pig, and that little pig," while she warmed our toes.

"Don't tell me!" said Aunt Trixie. Aunt Trixie never liked the Roderick Holabirds.

We tried not to think about it, but it was not comfortable. It was, indeed, a very serious anxiety and trouble that began, in consequence, to force itself upon us.

After the bright, gay nights had come weary, vexing days. And the worst was a vague shadow of family distrust and annoyance. Nobody thought any real harm, nobody disbelieved or suspected; but there it was. We could not think how such a declared determination and act of Grandfather Holabird should have come to nothing. Uncle and Aunt Roderick " could not see what we could expect about it; there was nothing to show; and there were John and John's children; it was not for any one or two to settle."

Only Ruth said " we were all good people, and meant right; it must all come right, somehow."

But father made up his mind that we could not afford to keep the place. He should pay his debts, now, the first thing. What was left must do for us; the house must go into the estate.

It was fixed, though, that we should stay there for the summer, — until affairs were settled.

" It 's a dumb shame!" said Aunt Trixie.

CHAPTER X.

RUTH'S RESPONSIBILITY.

HE June days did not make it any better. And the June nights, — well, we had to sit in the "front box at the sunset," and think how there would be June after June here for somebody, and we should only have had just two of them out of our whole lives.

Why did not grandfather give us that paper, when he began to ? And what could have become of it since ? And what if it were found some time, after the dear old place was sold and gone ? For it was the "dear old place " already to us, though we had only lived there a year, and though Aunt Roderick did say, in her cold fashion, just as if we could choose about it, that "it was not as if it were really an old homestead ; it would n't be so much of a change for us, if we made up our minds not to take it in, as if we had always lived there."

Why, we *had* always lived there! That was just the way we had always been trying to spell "home," though we had never got the right letters to do it with before. When exactly the right thing comes to you, it is a thing that has always been. You don't get the very sticks and stones to begin with, maybe; but what they stand for grows up in you, and when you come to it you know it is yours. The best things — the most glorious and wonderful of all — will be what we shall see to have been "laid up for us from the foundation." Aunt Roderick did not see one bit of how that was with us.

"There is n't a word in the tenth commandment about not coveting your *own* house," Barbara would say, boldly. And we did covet, and we did grieve. And although we did not mean to have "hard thoughts," we felt that Aunt Roderick was hard; and that Uncle Roderick and Uncle John were hatefully matter-of-fact and of-course about the "business." And that paper might be somewhere, yet. We did not believe that Grandfather Holabird had "changed his mind and burned it up." He had not had much mind to change, within those last six months. When he *was* well, and had a mind, we knew what he had meant to do.

If Uncle Roderick and Uncle John had not believed a word of what father told them, they could not have behaved very differently. We half thought, sometimes, that they did not believe it. And very likely they half thought that we were making it appear that they had done something that was not right. And it is the half

thoughts that are the **hard** thoughts. " It is very dis-
agreeable," Aunt Roderick **used to say.**

Miss Trixie Spring came over **and** spent days with us,
as of old ; and when the house looked sweet and pleasant
with the shaded summer light, and was full of the gracious
summer freshness, she would look round and shake her
head, **and say,** " **It 's** just as beautiful as it can **be.** And
it 's a **dumb shame.** Don't tell *me!* "

Uncle Roderick was going to " take in " the old homestead with **his** share, and that was as much as he cared
about ; Uncle John was used to nothing but stocks and
railway shares, and did **not want** " encumbrances " ; and
as to keeping it as estate property and **paying** rent to the
heirs, ourselves included, — nobody wanted that ; they
would rather have things settled up. There would always
be questions of estimates **and** repairs ; **it** was not best to
have things so **in a** family. Separate accounts as well as
short ones, made best friends. We knew they all thought
father was unlucky to have to do with in such matters.
He would still **be** the " limited " man of the family. It
would take two thirds of his inheritance to pay off **those**
old '57 debts.

So **we took our** lovely Westover summer days **as** things
we could not have any more of. And **when** you begin
to feel that **about** anything, **it** would be a relief to have
had the last of **it.** Nothing lasts always ; but we like to
have the forever-and-ever feeling, however delusive. A
child hates his Sunday clothes, because he knows he cannot put them on again on Monday.

With all our troubles, there was one pleasure in the
house, — Arctura. We had made an art-kitchen ; now

we were making a little poem of a serving-maiden. We did not turn things over to her, and so leave chaos to come again; we only let her help; we let her come in and learn with us the nice and pleasant ways that we had learned. We did not move the kitchen down stairs again; we were determined not to have a kitchen any more.

Arctura was strong and blithe; she could fetch and carry, make fires, wash dishes, clean knives and brasses, do all that came hardest to us; and could do, in other things, with and for us, what she saw us do. We all worked together till the work was done; then Arctura sat down in the afternoons, just as we did, and read books, or made her clothes. She always looked nice and pretty. She had large dark calico aprons for her work; and little white bib-aprons for table-tending and dress-up; and mother made for her, on the machine, little linen collars and cuffs.

We had a pride in her looks; and she knew it; she learned to work as delicately as we did. When breakfast or dinner was ready, she was as fit to turn round and serve as we were to sit down; she was astonished herself, at ways and results that she fell in with and attained.

"Why, where does the dirt go to?" she would exclaim. "It never gethers anywheres."

"GATHERS, — *anywhere*," Rosamond corrected.

Arctura learned little grammar lessons, and other such things, by the way. She was only "next" below us in our family life; there was no great gulf fixed. We felt that we had at least got hold of the right end of one thread in the social tangle. This, at any rate, had come out of our year at Westover.

" Things seem so easy," the girl would say. " It is just like two times one."

So it was ; because we did not jumble in all the Analysis and Compound Proportion of housekeeping right on top of the multiplication-table. She would get on by degrees ; by and by she would be in evolution and geometrical progression without knowing how she got there. If you want a house, you must build it up, stone by stone, and stroke by stroke ; if you want a servant, you, or somebody for you, must *build* one, just the same ; they do not spring up and grow, neither can be " knocked together." And I tell you, busy, eager women of this day, wanting great work out of doors, this is just what " we girls," some of us, — and some of the best of us, perhaps, — have got to stay at home awhile and do.

" It is one of the little jobs that has been waiting for a good while to be done," says Barbara ; " and Miss Pennington has found out another. ' There may be,' she says, ' need of women for reorganizing town-meetings ; I won't undertake to say there is n't ; but I 'm *sure* there 's need of them for reorganizing *parlor* meetings. They are getting to be left altogether to the little schoolgirl " sets." Women who have grown older, and can see through all that nonsense, and have the position and power to break it up, ought to take hold. Don't you think so ? Don't you think it is the duty of women of my age and class to see to this thing before it grows any worse ?' And I told her, — right up, respectful, — Yes 'm ; it wum ! Think of her asking me, though ! "

Just as things were getting to be so different and so nice on West Hill, it seemed so hard to leave it ! Everything reminded us of that.

A beautiful plan came up for Ruth, though, at this time. What with the family worries, — which Ruth always had a way of gathering to herself, and hugging up, prickers in, as if so she could keep the nettles from other people's fingers, — and her hard work at her music, she was getting thin. We were all insisting that she must take a vacation this summer, both from teaching and learning; when, all at once, Miss Pennington made up her mind to go to West Point and Lake George, and to take Penelope with her; and she came over and asked Ruth to go too.

"If you don't mind a room alone, dear; I 'm an awful coward to have come of a martial family, and I must have Pen with me nights. I 'm nervous about cars, too; I want two of you to keep up a chatter; I should be miserable company for one, always distracted after the whistles."

Ruth's eyes shone; but she colored up, and her thanks had half a doubt in them. She would tell Auntie: and they would think how it could be.

"What a nice way for you to go!" said Barbara, after Miss Pennington left. "And how nice it will be for you to see Dakie!" At which Ruth colored up again, and only said that "it would certainly be the nicest possible way to go, if she were to go at all."

Barbara meant — or meant to be understood that she meant — that Miss Pennington knew everybody, and belonged among the general officers; Ruth had an instinct that it would only be possible for her to go by an invitation like this from people out of her own family.

"But does n't it seem queer she should choose me, out

of us all?" she asked.   "Does n't it seem selfish for me
to be the one to go?"

"Seem selfish?   Whom to?" said Barbara, bluntly.
"We were n't asked."

" I wish—everybody—knew that," said Ruth.

Making this little transparent speech, Ruth blushed
once more. But she went, after all. She said we pushed
her out of the nest. She went out into the wide, wonderful world, for the very first time in her life.

This is one of her letters : —

DEAR MOTHER AND GIRLS: — It is perfectly lovely
here. I wish you could sit where I do this morning, looking up the still river in the bright light, with the tender purple haze on the far-off hills, and long, low, shady Constitution Island lying so beautiful upon the water on one side,
and dark shaggy Cro' Nest looming up on the other. The
Parrott guns at the foundry, over on the headland opposite, are trying,— as they are trying almost all the time, —
against the face of the high, old, desolate cliff; and the
hurtling buzz of the shells keeps a sort of slow, tremendous time-beat on the air.

I think I am almost more interested in Constitution Isl-
and than in any other part of the place. I never knew
until I came here that it was the home of the Misses War-
ner; the place where Queechy came from, and Dollars
and Cents, and the Wide, Wide World. It seems so
strange to think that they sit there and write still, lovely
stories while all this parade and bustle and learning how to
fight are going on close beside and about them.

The Cadets are very funny. They will do almost any

thing for mischief, — the frolic of it, I mean. Dakie
Thayne tells us very amusing stories. They are just going into camp now ; and they have parades and battery-
practice every day. They have target-firing at old Cro'
Nest, — which has to stand all the firing from the north
battery, just around here from the hotel. One day the
cadet in charge made a very careful sighting of his piece ;
made the men train the gun up and down, this way and
that, a hair more or a hair less, till they were nearly out
of patience ; when, lo! just as he had got "a beautiful
bead," round came a superintending officer, and took a
look too. The bad boy had drawn it full on a poor old
black cow ! I do not believe he would have really let her
be blown up ; but Dakie says, — "Well, he rather
thinks, — if she would have stood still long enough, — he
would have let her be — astonished ! "

The walk through the woods, around the cliff, over the
river, is beautiful. If only they would n't call it by such
a silly name !

We went out to Old Fort Putnam yesterday. I did not
know how afraid Miss Pennington could be of a little
thing before. I don't know, now, how much of it was
fun ; for, as Dakie Thayne said, it was agonizingly funny.
What must have happened to him after we got back
and he left us I cannot imagine ; he did n't laugh much
there, and it must have been a misery of politeness.

We had been down into the old, ruinous enclosure ;
had peeped in at the dark, choked-up casemates ; and had
gone round and come up on the edge of the broken em-
bankment, which we were following along to where it
sloped down safely again, — when, just at the very mid-

dle and highest and most impossible point, down sat Miss
Elizabeth among the stones, and declared she could neither go back nor forward. She had been frightened to death
all the way, and now her head was quite gone. "No;
nothing should persuade her; she never could get up on
her feet again in that dreadful place." She laughed in
the midst of it; but she was really frightened, and there
she sat; Dakie went to her, and tried to help her up, and
lead her on; but she would not be helped. "What
would come of it?" "She did n't know; she supposed
that was the end of her; *she* could n't do anything."
"But, dear Miss Pennington," says Dakie, "are you going to break short off with life, right here, and make a
Lady Simon Stylites of yourself?" "For all she knew;
she never could get down." I think we must have been
there, waiting and coaxing, nearly half an hour, before she
began to *hitch* along; for walk she would n't, and she did
n't. She had on a black Ernani dress, and a nice silk
underskirt; and as she lifted herself along with her hands,
hoist after hoist sidewise, of course the thin stuff dragged on
the rocks and began to go to pieces. By the time she came
to where she could stand, she was a rebus of the Coliseum,
— "a noble wreck in ruinous perfection." She just had
to tear off the long tatters, and roll them up in a bunch,
and fling them over into a hollow, and throw the two
or three breadths that were left over her arm, and walk
home in her silk petticoat, itself much the sufferer from
dust and fray, though we did all we could for her with
pocket-handkerchiefs.

"What *has* happened to Miss Pennington?" said Mrs.
General M——, as we came up on the piazza.

"Nothing," said Dakie, quite composed and proper, "only she got tired and sat down ; and it was dusty, — that was all." He bowed and went off, without so much as a glance of secret understanding.

"A joke has as many lives as a cat, here," he told Pen and me, afterwards, "and that was *too* good not to keep to ourselves."

Dear little mother and girls, — I have told stories and described describes, and all to crowd out and leave to the last corner *such* a thing that Dakie Thayne wants to do ! We got to talking about Westover and last summer, and the pleasant old place, and all ; and I could n't help telling him something about the worry. I know I had no business to ; and I am afraid I have made a snarl. He says he would like to buy the place ! And he wanted to know if Uncle Stephen would n't rent it of him if he did ! Just think of it, — that boy ! I believe he really means to write to Chicago, to his guardian. Of course it never came into my head when I told him ; it would n't at any rate, and I never think of *his* having such a quantity of money. He seems just like — as far as that goes — any other boy. What shall I do ? Do you believe he will ?

P. S. Saturday morning. I feel better about that Poll Parroting of mine, to-day. I have had another talk with Dakie. I don't believe he will write ; now, at any rate. O girls ! this is just the most perfect morning !

Tell Stephen I 've got a *splendid* little idea, on purpose for him and me. Something I can hardly keep to myself till I get home. Dakie Thayne put it into my head. He is just the brightest boy, about everything ! I begin to feel in a hurry almost, to come back.   I don't think Miss Pennington will go to Lake George, after all. She says she hates to leave the Point, so many of her old friends are here.   But Pen and I think she is afraid of the steamers.

Ruth got home a week after this ; a little fatter, a little browner, and a little merrier and more talkative than she had ever been before.

Stephen was in a great hurry about the splendid little mysterious idea, of course.   Boys never can wait, half so well as girls, for anything.

We were all out on the balcony that night before dusk, as usual. Ruth got up suddenly, and went into the house for something. Stephen went straight in after her.   What happened upon that, the rest of us did not know till afterward.   But it is a nice little part of the story, — just because there is so precious little of it.

Ruth went round, through the brown room and the hall, to the front door. Stephen found her stooping down, with her face close to the piazza cracks.

" Hollo ! what's the matter ?   Lost something ? "

Ruth lifted up her head.   " Hush ! "

" Why, how your face shines !   What *is* up ? "

" It 's the sunset.   I mean — that shines.   Don't say anything.   Our splendid — little — idea, you know.   It 's under here."

" Be dar — never-minded, if mine is ! "

" You don't know.   Columbus did n't know where his idea was — exactly.   Do you remember when Sphinx hid her kittens under here last summer ?   Brought 'em round,

over the wood-pile in the shed, and they never knew their
way out till she showed 'em ?"

" It *is n't* about kittens !"

" Has n't Old Ma'amselle got some now ?"

" Yes ; four."

" Could n't you bring up one — or two — to-morrow
morning *early*, and make a place and tuck 'em in here,
under the step, and put back the sod, and fasten 'em up ?"

" What — *for ?*" with wild amazement.

" I can't do what I want to, just for an idea. It will
make a noise, and I don't feel sure enough. There had
better be a kitten. I 'll tell you the rest to-morrow morning." And Ruth was up on her two little feet, and had
given Stephen a kiss, and was back into the house, and
round again to the balcony, before he could say another
word.

Boys like a plan, though ; especially a mysterious getting-
up-early plan ; and if it has cats in it, it is always funny.
He made up his mind to be on hand.

Ruth was first, though. She kept her little bolt drawn
all night, between her room and that of Barbara and Rose.
At five o'clock, she went softly across the passage to Stephen's room, in her little wrapper and knit slippers. " I
shall be ready in ten minutes," she whispered, right into
his ear, and into his dream.

" Scat ! " cried Stephen, starting up bewildered.

And Ruth " scatted."

Down on the front piazza, twenty minutes after, she
superintended the tucking in of the kittens, and then told
him to bring a mallet and wedge. She had been very
particular to have the kittens put under at a precise place,

though there was a ready-made hole farther on. The cat babies mewed and sprawled **and** dragged themselves at **feeble** length **on** their miserable little legs, as small blind kittiewinks are given **to** doing.

"They **won't go far,**" said Ruth. "**Now, let 's take** this board **up.**"

"**What** — *for ?* " **cried** Stephen, again.

"**To get them out,** of course," says Ruth.

"**Well, if** girls ain't queer! Queerer than cats!"

"**Hush !**" said Ruth, softly. "I *believe* — **but** I don't dare say a word yet — there 's something there!"

"Of course there is. Two little yowling—"

"Something we all want found, Steve," Ruth whispered, earnestly. "**But I don't** know. **Do** hush! Make haste!"

Stephen put **down his face to the crack, and** took a peep. Rather **a** long serious peep. When he took his face back again, "I *see* something," he said. "It 's white paper. Kind of white, that is. Do you suppose, Ruth — ? My cracky! if you do!"

"**We** won't suppose," said Ruth. "**We 'll** hammer."

Stephen **knocked up** the end of the board with the mallet, **and then he got the** wedge under **and** pried. **Ruth pulled.** Stephen kept hammering and prying, and Ruth **held** on **to** all **he gained,** until they slipped the wedge along gradually, to where the board **was** nailed again, to **the** middle joist or stringer. Then a few more vigorous strokes, and a little smart levering, and the nails loosened, and one good wrench lifted it from the inside timber and they slid it out from under the house-boarding.

Underneath **lay a long,** folded paper, **much** covered

with drifts of dust, and speckled somewhat with damp. But it was a dry, sandy place, and weather had not badly injured it.

"Stephen, I am sure!" said Ruth, holding Stephen back by the arm. "Don't touch it, though! Let it be, right there. Look at that corner, that lies opened up a little. Is n't that grandfather's writing?"

It lay deep down, and not directly under. They could scarcely have reached it with their hands. Stephen ran into the parlor, and brought out an opera-glass that was upon the table there.

"That's bright of you, Steve!" cried Ruth.

Through the glass they discerned clearly the handwriting. They read the words, at the upturned corner, — "heirs after him."

"Lay the board back in its place," said Ruth. "It is n't for us to meddle with any more. Take the kittens away." Ruth had turned quite pale.

Going down to the barn with Stephen, presently, carrying the two kittens in her arms, while he had the mallet and wedge, —

"Stephen," said she, "I 'm going to do something on my own responsibility."

"I should think you had."

"O, that was nothing. I had to do that. I had to make sure before I said anything. But now, — I 'm going to ask Uncle and Aunt Roderick to come over. They ought to be here, you know."

"Why! don't you suppose they will believe, now?"

"Stephen Holabird! you 're a bad boy! No; of course it is n't that." Ruth kept right on from the barn, across the field, into the "old place."

Mrs. Roderick Holabird was out in the east piazza, watering her house plants, that stood in a row against the wall. Her cats always had their milk, and her plants their water, before she had her own breakfast. It was a good thing about Mrs. Roderick Holabird, and it was a good time to take her.

"Aunt Roderick," said Ruth, coming up, "I want you and Uncle to come over right after breakfast; or before, if you like; if you please."

It was rather sudden, but for the repeated "ifs."

" *You* want ! " said Mrs. Roderick in surprise. " Who sent you ? "

" Nobody. Nobody knows but Stephen and me. Something is going to happen." Ruth smiled, as one who has a pleasant astonishment in store. She smiled right up out of her heart-faith in Aunt Roderick and everybody.

" On the whole, I guess you 'd better come right off, — *to* breakfast ! " How boldly little Ruth took the responsibility ! Mr. and Mrs. Roderick had not been over to our house for at least two months. It had seemed to happen so. Father always went there to attend to the " business." The " papers " were all at grandfather's. All but this one, that the " gale " had taken care of.

Uncle Roderick, hearing the voices, came out into the piazza.

" We want you over at our house," repeated Ruth. " Right off, now ; there 's something you ought to see about."

" I don't like mysteries," said Mrs. Roderick, severely, covering her curiosity ; " especially when children get them up. And it 's no matter about the breakfast, either way. We can walk across, I suppose, Mr. Holabird, and see what it is all about. Kittens, I dare say."

" Yes," said Ruth, laughing out ; " it *is* kittens, partly. Or was."

So we saw them, from mother's room window, all coming along down the side-hill path together.

We always went out at the front door to look at the morning. Arctura had set the table, and baked the biscuits ; we could breathe a little first breath of life, nowadays, that did not come cut of the oven.

12

Father was in the door-way. Stephen stood, as if he had been put there, over the loose board, that we did not know was loose.

Ruth brought Uncle and Aunt Roderick up the long steps, and so around.

" Good morning," said father, surprised. " Why, Ruth, what is it? " And he met them right on that very loose board ; and Stephen stood stock still, pertinaciously in the way, so that they dodged and blundered about him.

" Yes, Ruth ; what is it? " said Mrs. Roderick Holabird.

Then Ruth, after she had got the family solemnly together, began to be struck with the solemnity. Her voice trembled.

" I did n't mean to make a fuss about it ; only I knew you would all care, and I wanted — Stephen and I have found something, mother ! " She turned to Mrs. Stephen Holabird, and took her hand, and held it hard.

Stephen stooped down, and drew out the loose board. " Under there," said he ; and pointed in.

They could all see the folded paper, with the drifts of dust upon it, just as it had lain for almost a year.

" It has been there ever since the day of the September Gale, father," he said. " The day, you know, that grandfather was here."

" Don't you remember the wind and the papers ? " said Ruth. " It was remembering that, that put it into our heads. I never thought of the cracks and — " with a little, low, excited laugh — " the ' total depravity of inanimate things,' till — just a little while ago."

She did not say a word about that bright boy at West Point, now, before them all.

Uncle Roderick reached in with the crook of his cane, and drew forward the packet, and stooped down and lifted it up. He shook off the dust and opened it. He glanced along the lines, and at the signature. Not a single witnessing name. No matter. Uncle Roderick is an honest man. He turned round and held it out to father.

"It is your deed of gift," said he; and then they two shook hands.

"There!" said Ruth, tremulous with gladness. "I knew they would. That was it. That was why. I told you, Stephen!"

"No, you did n't," said Stephen. "You never told me anything — but cats."

"Well! I 'm sure I am glad it is all settled," said Mrs. Roderick Holabird, after a pause; "and nobody has any hard thoughts to lay up."

They would not stop to breakfast; they said they would come another time.

But Aunt Roderick, just before she went away, turned round and kissed Ruth. She is a supervising, regulating kind of a woman, and very strict about — well, other people's — expenditures; but she was glad that the "hard thoughts" were lifted off from her.

"I knew," said Ruth, again, "that we were all good people, and that it must come right."

"Don't tell me!" says Miss Trixie, intolerantly. "She could n't help herself."

CHAPTER XI.

BARBARA'S BUZZ.

ESLIE GOLDTHWAITE'S world of friendship is not a circle. Or if it is, it is the far-off, immeasurable horizon that holds all of life and possibility.

"You must draw the line somewhere," people say. "You cannot be acquainted with everybody."

But Leslie's lines are only radii. They reach out to wherever there is a sympathy; they hold fast wherever they have once been joined. Consequently, she moves to laws that seem erratic to those for whom a pair of compasses can lay down the limit. Consequently, her wedding was "odd."

If Olivia Marchbanks had been going to be married there would have been a "circle" invited. Nobody would have been left out; nobody would have been let in. She had lived in this necromantic ring; she would be married in it ; she would die and be buried in it ; and of all the wide, rich, beautiful champaign of life beyond, — of all its noble heights, and hidden, tender hollows, — its gracious harvest fields, and its deep, grand, forest glooms, — she would be content, elegantly and exclusively, to know nothing. To her wedding people might come, indeed, from a distance, — geographically ; but they would come out of a precisely corresponding little sphere in some other place, and fit right into this one, for the time being, with the most edifying sameness.

From the east and the west, the north and the south, they began to come, days beforehand, — the people who could not let Leslie Goldthwaite be married without being there. There were no proclamation cards issued, bearing in imposing characters the announcement of "Their Daughter's Marriage," by Mr. and Mrs. Aaron Goldthwaite, after the like of which one almost looks to see, and somewhat feels the need of, the regular final invocation, — "God save the Commonwealth!"

There had been loving letters sent here and there ; old Miss Craydocke, up in the mountains, got one, and came down a month earlier in consequence, and by the way of Boston. She stayed there at Mrs. Frank Scherman's ; and Frank and his wife and little Sinsie, the baby, — "she is n't Original Sin, as I was," says her mother, — came up to Z—— together, and stopped at the hotel. Martha Josselyn came from New York, and stayed, of course, with the Inglesides.

Martha is a horrible thing, girls ; how do you suppose I dare to put her in here as I do ? She is a milliner. And this is how it happens. Her father is a compara-

tively poor man, — a book-keeper with a salary. There
are ever so many little Josselyns ; and Martha has always
felt bound to help. She is not very likely to marry, and
she is not one to take it into her calculation, if she were ;
but she is of the sort who are said to be " cut out for old
maids," and she knows it. She could not teach music,
nor keep a school, her own schooling — not her educa-
tion ; God never lets that be cut short — was abridged
by the need of her at home. But she could do anything
in the world with scissors and needle; and she can make
just the loveliest bonnets that ever were put together.

So, as she can help more by making two bonnets in a
day, and getting six dollars for them beside the materials,
she lets her step-mother put out her impossible sewing,
and has turned a little second-story room in her father's
house into a private millinery establishment. She will
only take the three dollars apiece, beyond the actual cost,
for her bonnets, although she might make a fortune if
she would be rapacious ; for she says that pays her fairly
for her time, and she has made up her mind to get
through the world fairly, if there is any breathing-space
left for fairness in it. If not, she can stop breathing, and
go where there is.

She gets as much to do as she can take. " Miss Josselyn " is one of the little unadvertised resources of New
York, which it is very knowing, and rather elegant, to
know about. But it would not be at all elegant to have
her at a party. Hence, Mrs. Van Alstyne, who had a
little bonnet, of black lace and nasturtiums, at this very
time, that Martha Josselyn had made for her, was astonished to find that she was Mrs. Ingleside's sister and had
come on to the marriage.

General and Mrs. Ingleside — Leslie's cousin Delight — had come from their away-off, beautiful Wisconsin home, and brought little three-year-old Rob and Rob's nurse with them. Sam Goldthwaite was at home from Phila-delphia, where he is just finishing his medical course, — and Harry was just back again from the Mediterranean; so that Mrs. Goldthwaite's house was full too. Jack could not be here; they all grieved over that. Jack is out in Japan. But there came a wonderful "solid silk" dress, and a lovely inlaid cabinet, for Leslie's wedding present, — the first present that arrived from anybody; sent the day he got the news; — and Leslie cried over them, and kissed them, and put the beautiful silk away, to be made up in the fashion next year, when Jack comes home; and set his picture on the cabinet, and put his letters into it, and says she does not know what other things she shall find quite dear enough to keep them company.

Last of all, the very day before the wedding, came old Mr. Marmaduke Wharne. And of all things in the world, he brought her a telescope. "To look out at creation with, and keep her soul wide," he says, and "to put her in mind of that night when he first found her out, among the Hivites and the Hittites and the Amalekites, up in Jefferson, and took her away among the planets, out of the snarl."

Miss Craydocke has been all summer making a fernery for Leslie; and she took two tickets in the cars, and brought it down beside her, on the seat, all the way from Plymouth, and so out here. How they could get it to wherever they are going we all wondered, but Dr.

Hautayne said it should **go ; he** would have it most curi-
ously packed, in **a** box **on** rollers, **and** marked, — " Dr.
J. Hautayne, U. S. Army.   Valuable scientific prepara-
tions ; **by** no means to be turned or shaken."   But he
did **say,** with **a** gentle prudence, — " If somebody should
give you an observatory, or a greenhouse, **I** think **we**
might **have to stop at** *that*, dear."

Nobody did, however.   There was only one more big
present, **and** that did not come.   Dakie Thayne knew
better.   He gave her a magnificent copy of the Sistine
Madonna, which his father had bought in Italy, and he
wrote her that it was to be boxed and sent after her to her
home.   *He* did **not** say **that** it was magnificent ; Leslie
wrote that to us afterward, herself.   She said **it** made it
seem as **if one** side of her little home had been broken
through and let in heaven.

We were all sorry that Dakie could not be here.   They
waited till September **for** Harry ; " but who," wrote Dakie, " could expect a military engagement to wait till all
the stragglers could come up ?   I have given my consent
and my blessing ; all I ask is that you will stop **at West**
Point on your way."   **And that was what they were
going to do.**

Arabel Waite and Delia **made all the** wedding dresses.
But **Mrs.** Goldthwaite had her own carefully perfected
patterns, adjusted to a line in every part.   Arabel meekly
followed these, and saved her whole, fresh soul to pour
out upon the flutings and finishing.

It was a morning wedding, and a pearl of days.   The
summer had not gone from a single leaf.   Only the parch
and the blaze were over, and beautiful dews had cooled

away their fever. The day-lilies were white among their broad, tender green leaves, and the tube-roses had come in blossom. There were beds of red and white carnations, heavy with perfume. The wide garden porch, into which double doors opened from the summer-room where they were married, showed these, among the grass-walks of the shady, secluded place, through its own splendid vista of trumpet-hung bignonia vines.

Everybody wanted to help at this wedding who could help. Arabel Waite asked to be allowed to pour out coffee, or something. So in a black silk gown, and a new white cap, she took charge of the little room up stairs, where were coffee and cakes and sandwiches for the friends who came from a distance by the train, and might be glad of something to eat at twelve o'clock. Delia offered, " if she only might," to assist in the dining-room, where the real wedding collation stood ready. And even our Arctura came and asked if she might be " lent," to " open doors, or anything." The regular maids of the house found labor so divided that it was a festival day all through.

Arctura looked as pretty a little waiting-damsel as might be seen, in her brown, two-skirted, best delaine dress, and her white, ruffled, muslin bib-apron, her nicely arranged hair, braided up high around her head and frizzed a little, gently, at the front, — since why should n't she, too, have a bit of the fashion? — and tied round with a soft, simple white ribbon. Delia had on a violet-and-white striped pique, quite new, with a ruffled apron also; and her ribbon was white, too, and she had a bunch of violets and green leaves upon her bosom. We cared as

much about their dress as they did about ours.   Barbara
herself had pinched **Arctura's crimps, and** tied the little
white **bow among them.**

Every room **in the house was** attended.

"There **never was** such pretty serving," said **Mrs.
Van Alstyne, afterward.** "Where *did* they get **such peo-**
ple? — **And** beautiful serving," she went on, reverting
to her favorite axiom, " is, after **all,** the very soul **of liv-**
ing!"

"Yes, ma'am," said Barbara, **gravely.** "I think **we**
shall find that true **always."**

Opposite the **door into** the garden **porch were corre-**
sponding ones into **the** hall, and **directly down to** these
reached **the last** flight of the staircase, that skirted the
walls at the back with its steps and landings.   We could
see Leslie all the way, as she came down, with her hand
in her father's arm.

She descended beside **him** like **a** softly accompanying
white cloud ; her dress was of tulle, without a hitch or **a**
puff or a festoon about it.   It had two skirts, I believe,
but **they were** plain-hemmed, and fell like **a mist about**
her figure.   Underneath was **no rustling silk, or shining**
satin ; only more mist, **of finest, sheerest quaker-muslin ;**
you could not tell where the cloud met the opaque **of**
soft, unstarched cambric below **it all.**   And from her head
to her feet floated **the** shimmering veil, fastened **to** her
hair with only two **or** three tube-rose blooms and the
green leaves and white stars of the larger myrtle.   There
was a cluster of them upon her bosom, and she held some
in her left hand.

Dr. Hautayne looked nobly handsome, as he came forward to her side in his military dress; but I think we all had another picture of him in our minds, — dusty, and battle-stained, bareheaded, in his shirt-sleeves, as he rode across the fire to save men's lives. When a man has once looked like that, it does not matter how he ever merely *looks* again.

Marmaduke Wharne stood close by Ruth, during the service. She saw his gray, shaggy brows knit themselves into a low, earnest frown, as he fixedly watched and listened; but there was a shining underneath, as still waterdrops shine under the gray moss of some old, cleft rock; and a pleasure upon the lines of the rough-cast face, that was like the tender glimmering of a sunbeam.

When Marmaduke Wharne first saw John Hautayne, he put his hand upon his shoulder, and held him so, while he looked him hardly in the face.

"Do you think you deserve her, John?" the old man said. And John looked him back, and answered straightly, "No!" It was not mere apt and effective reply; there was an honest heartful on the lips and in the eyes; and Leslie's old friend let his hand slip down along the strong, young arm, until it grasped the answering hand, and said again, —

"Perhaps, then, John, — you 'll do!"

"Who giveth this woman to be married to this man?" That is what the church asks, in her service, though nobody asked it here to-day. But we all felt we had a share to give of what we loved so much. Her father and her mother gave; her girl friends gave; Miss Trixie Spring, Arabel Waite, Delia, little Arctura, the home-servants, gathered in the door-way, all gave; Miss Craydocke, cry-

ing, and disdaining her pocket-handkerchief till the tears trickled off her chin, because she was smiling also and would not cover *that* up, — gave ; and nobody gave with a more loving wrench out of a deep heart, than bluff old frowning Marmaduke Wharne.

Nobody knows the comfort that we Holabirds took, though, in those autumn days, after all this was over, in our home ; feeling every bright, comfortable minute, that our home was our own. "It is so nice to have it to love grandfather by," said Ruth, like a little child.

"Everything is so pleasant," said Barbara, one sumptuous morning. "I 've so many nice things that I can choose among to do. I feel like a bee in a barrel of sugar. I don't know where to begin." Barbara had a new dress to make; she had also a piece of worsted work to begin; she had also two new books to read aloud, that Mrs. Scherman had brought up from Boston.

We felt rich in much prospectively; we could afford things better now; we had proposed and arranged a book-club; Miss Pennington and we were to manage it; Mrs. Scherman was to purchase for us. Ruth was to have plenty of music. Life was full and bright to us, this golden autumn-time, as it had never been before. The time itself was radiant; and the winter was stored beforehand with pleasures; Arctura was as glad as anybody; she hears our readings in the afternoons, when she can come up stairs, and sit mending stockings or hemming aprons.

We knew, almost for the first time, what it was to be without any pressure of anxiety. We dared to look round the house and see what was wearing out. We could re-place things — *some*, at any rate — as well as not; so we had the delight of choosing, and the delight of putting by; it was a delicious perplexity. We all felt like Barbara's bee; and when she said that once she said it for every day, all through the new and happy time.

It was wonderful how little there was, after all, that we did want in any hurry. We thought it over. We did not care to carpet the dining-room; we liked the drugget and the dark wood-margins better. It came down pretty nearly, at last, so far as household improvements were con-cerned, to a new broadcloth cover for the great family table in the brown-room.

Barbara's *bee*-havior, however, had its own queer fluc-
tuations at this time, it must be confessed. Whatever
the reason was, it was not altogether to be depended on.
It had its alternations of humming content with a good
deal of whimsical bouncing and buzzing and the most un-
predictable flights. To use a phrase of Aunt Trixie's
applied to her childhood, but coming into new appropri-
ateness now, Barbara " acted like a witch."

She began at the wedding. Only a minute or two
before Leslie came down, Harry Goldthwaite moved over
to where she stood just a little apart from the rest of us,
by the porch door, and placed himself beside her, with
some little commonplace word in a low tone, as befitted
the hushed expectancy of the moment.

All at once, with an " O, I forgot! " she started away
from him in the abruptest fashion, and glanced off across
the room, and over into a little side parlor beyond the
hall, into which she certainly had not been before that
day. She could have " forgotten " nothing there; but
she doubtless had just enough presence of mind not to
rush up the staircase toward the dressing-rooms, at the
risk of colliding with the bridal party. When Leslie an
instant later came in at the double doors, Mrs. Holabird
caught sight of Barbara again just sliding into the far,
lower corner of the room by the forward entrance, where
she stood looking out meekly between the shoulders and
the floating cap-ribbons of Aunt Trixie Spring and Miss
Arabel Waite during the whole ceremony.

Whether it was that she felt there was something
dangerous in the air, or that Harry Goldthwaite had
some new awfulness in her eyes from being actually a

commissioned officer, — Ensign Goldthwaite, now, (Rose had borrowed from the future, for the sake of euphony and effect, when she had so retorted feet and dignities upon her last year,) — we could not guess; but his name or presence seemed all at once a centre of electrical disturbances in which her whisks and whirls were simply to be wondered at.

"I don't see why he should tell *me* things," was what she said to Rosamond one day, when she took her to task after Harry had gone, for making off almost before he had done speaking, when he had been telling us of the finishing of some business that Mr. Goldthwaite had managed for him in Newburyport. It was the sale of a piece of property that he had there, from his father, of houses and building-lots that had been unprofitable to hold, because of uncertain tenants and high taxes, but which were turned now into a comfortable round sum of money.

"I shall not be so poor now, as if I had only my pay," said Harry. At which Barbara had disappeared.

"Why, you were both there!" said Barbara.

"Well, yes; we were there in a fashion. He was sitting by you, though, and he looked up at you, just then. It did not seem very friendly."

"I'm sure I did n't notice; I don't see why he should tell me things," said whimsical Barbara.

"Well, perhaps he will stop," said Rose, quietly, and walked away.

It seemed, after a while, as if he would. He could not understand Barbara in these days. All her nice, cordial, honest ways were gone. She was always shying

at something. Twice he was here, when she did not
come into the room until tea-time.

"There are so many people," she said, in her unrea-
sonable manner. "They make me nervous, looking and
listening."

We had Miss Craydocke and Mrs. Scherman with us
then. We had asked them to come and spend a week
with us before they left Z——.

Miss Craydocke had found Barbara one evening, in the
twilight, standing alone in one of the brown-room windows. She had come up, in her gentle, old-friendly way,
and stood beside her.

"My dear," she said, with the twilight impulse of
nearness, — "I am an old woman. Are n't you pushing
something away from you, dear ?"

"Ow !" said Barbara, as if Miss Craydocke had pinched
her. And poor Miss Craydocke could only walk away
again.

When it came to Aunt Roderick, though, it was too
much. Aunt Roderick came over a good deal now.
She had quite taken us into unqualified approval again,
since we had got the house. She approved herself also.
As if it was she who had died and left us something, and
looked back upon it now with satisfaction. At least, as
if she had been the September Gale, and had taken care
of that paper for us.

Aunt Roderick has very good practical eyes ; but no
sentiment whatever. "It seems to me, Barbara, that
you are throwing away your opportunities," she said,
plainly.

Barbara looked up with a face of bold unconsciousness.

She was brought to bay, now; Aunt Roderick could exasperate her, but she could not touch the nerve, as dear Miss Craydocke could.

"I always am throwing them away," said Barbara. "It's my fashion. I never could save corners. I always put my pattern right into the middle of my piece, and the other half never comes out, you see. What have I done, now? Or what do you think I might do, just at present?"

"I think you might save yourself from being sorry by and by," said Aunt Roderick.

"I'm ever so much obliged to you," said Barbara, collectedly. "Just as much as if I could understand. But perhaps there'll be some light given. I'll turn it over in my mind. In the mean while, Aunt Roderick, I just begin to see one very queer thing in the world. You've lived longer than I have; I wish you could explain it. There are some things that everybody is very delicate about, and there are some that they take right hold of. People might have *pocket*-perplexities for years and years, and no created being would dare to hint or ask a question; but the minute it is a case of heart or soul, — or they think it is, — they 'rush right in where angels fear to tread.' What *do* you suppose makes the difference?"

After that, we all let her alone, behave as she might. We saw that there could be no meddling without marring. She had been too conscious of us all, before anybody spoke. We could only hope there was no real mischief done, already.

"It's all of them, every one!" she repeated, half

hysterically, that day, after her shell had exploded, and
Aunt Roderick had retreated, really with great forbear-
ance. "Miss Craydocke began, and I had to scream at
her; even Sin Scherman made a little moral speech
about her own wild ways, and set that baby crowing
over me! And once Aunt Trixie 'vummed' at me.
And I'm sure I ain't doing a single thing!" She whim-
pered and laughed, like a little naughty boy, called to
account for mischief, and pretending surprised innocence,
yet secretly at once enjoying and repenting his own
badness; and so we had to let her alone.

But after a while Harry Goldthwaite stayed away four
whole days, and then he only came in to say that he was
going to Washington to be gone a week. It was October,
now, and his orders might come any day. Then we
might not see him again for three years, perhaps.

On the Thursday of that next week, Barbara said she
would go down and see Mrs. Goldthwaite.

" I think it quite time you should," said Mrs. Holabird.
Barbara had not been down there once since the wedding-
day.

She put her crochet in her pocket, and we thought of
course she would stay to tea. It was four in the afternoon when she went away.

About an hour later Olivia Marchbanks called.

It came out that Olivia had a move to make. In fact,
that she wanted to set us all to making moves. She proposed a chess-club, for the winter, to bring us together
regularly; to include half a dozen families, and meet by
turn at the different houses.

"I dare say Miss Pennington will have her neighbor-

hood parties again," she said ; "they are nice, but rather
exhausting ; we want something quiet, to come in between. Something a little more among ourselves, you
know. Maria Hendee is a splendid chess-player, and so
is Mark. Maud plays with her father, and Adelaide and
I are learning. I know you play, Rosamond, and Barbara, — does n't she ? Nobody can complain of a chess-club,
you see ; and we can have a table at whist for the elders
who like it, and almost always a round game for the odds
and ends. After supper, we can dance, or anything. Don't
you think it would do ? "

"I think it would do nicely for *one* thing," said Rose,
thoughtfully. "But don't let us allow it to be the *whole*
of our winter."

Olivia Marchbanks's face clouded. She had put forward
a little pawn of compliment toward us, as towards a good
point, perhaps, for tempting a break in the game. And
behold ! Rosamond's knight only leaped right over it,
facing honestly and alertly both ways.

"Chess would be good for nothing less than once a
week," said Olivia. "I came to you almost the very first,
out of the family," she added, with a little height in her
manner. "I hope you won't break it up."

"Break it up ! No, indeed ! We were all getting just
nicely joined together," replied Rosamond, ladylike with
perfect temper. "I think last winter was so *really good*,"
she went on ; "I should be sorry to break up what *that*
did ; that is all."

"I 'm willing enough to help in those ways," said
Olivia, condescendingly ; "but I think we might have
our *own* things, too."

"I don't know, Olivia," said Rosamond, slowly, "about these 'own things.' **They are** just what begin to puzzle **me.**"

It was the bravest thing our elegant Rosamond had **ever** done. Olivia Marchbanks was angry. She all but took back her **invitation.**

"Never **mind,**" she said, getting up to take **leave.** "**It** must **be some time** yet; I only mentioned it. Perhaps **we** had better **not try** to go beyond ourselves, after all. Such **things are sure to be** stupid unless everybody is really interested."

Rosamond stood in the hall-door, as she went down the steps and away. At the same moment, Barbara, flushed with an evidently hurried walk, **came in.** "Why! what makes **you** so red, **Rose?**" she said.

"Somebody **has been** snubbing somebody," replied **Rose,** holding **her** royal color, like her namesake, in the midst of a cool repose. "And I don't quite know whether it is Olivia Marchbanks or I."

"**A** color-question between Rose and Barberry!" said Ruth. "**What** have *you* been doing, Barbie? **Why** did n't **you stay to tea?**"

"I? I've been walking, of course. — That boy has got **home again,**" she added, **half aloud, to** Rosamond, **as they** went **up** stairs.

We knew very well that she must **have** been queer **to** Harry again. He would have been certain to walk home with her, if she would have let him. But — "all through the town, and up the hill, in the daylight! Or — stay to **tea** with *him* there, **and** make him come, in the dark! — And *if* he imagined that I knew!" We were as sure as if she had said it, that these were the things that were in her mind, and that these were what she had run away from. How she had done it we did not know ; we had no doubt it had been something awful.

The next morning nobody called. Father came home to dinner and said Mr. Goldthwaite had told him that Harry was under orders, — to the " Katahdin."

In the afternoon Barbara went out and nailed up the woodbines. Then she put on her hat, and took a great bundle that had been waiting for a week for somebody to carry, and said she would go round to South Hollow with it, to Mrs. Dockery.

" You will be tired to death. You are tired already, hammering at those vines," said mother, anxiously. Mothers cannot help daughters much in these buzzes.

" I want the exercise," said Barbara, turning away her face that was at once red and pale. " Pounding and stamping are good for me." Then she came back in a hurry, and kissed mother, and then she went away.

CHAPTER XII.

EMERGENCIES.

RS. HOBART has a "fire-gown." That is what she calls it; she made it for a fire, or for illness, or any night alarm; she never goes to bed without hanging it over a chair-back, within instant reach. It is of double, bright-figured flannel, with a double cape sewed on; and a flannel belt, also sewed on behind, and furnished, for fastening, with a big, reliable, easy-going button and button-hole. Up and down the front — not too near together — are more big, reliable, easy-going buttons and button-holes. A pair of quilted slippers with thick soles belong with this gown, and are laid beside it. Then Mrs. Hobart goes to bed in peace, and sleeps like the virgin who knows there is oil in her vessel.

If Mrs. Roger Marchbanks had known of Mrs. Hobart's

fire-gown, and what it had been made and waiting for, unconsciously, all these years, she might not have given those quiet orders to her discreet, well-bred parlor-maid, by which she was never to be " disengaged " when Mrs. Hobart called.

Mrs. Hobart has also a gown of very elegant black silk, with deep, rich border-folds of velvet, and a black camel's-hair shawl whose priceless margin comes up to within three inches of the middle ; and in these she has turned meekly away from Mrs. Marchbanks's vestibule, leaving her inconsequential card, many wondering times ; never doubting, in her simplicity, that Mrs. Marchbanks was really making pies, or doing up pocket-handkerchiefs ; only thinking how queer it was it always happened so with her.

In her fire-gown she was destined to go in.

Barbara came home dreadfully tired from her walk to Mrs. Dockery's, and went to bed at eight o'clock. When one of us does that, it always breaks up our evening early. Mother discovered that she was sleepy by nine, and by half past we were all in our beds. So we really had a fair half night of rest before the alarm came.

It was about one in the morning when Barbara woke, as people do who go to bed achingly tired, and sleep hungrily for a few eager hours.

" My gracious ! what a moon ! What ails it ? "

The room was full of red light.

Rosamond sat up beside her.

" Moon ! It 's fire ! "

Then they called Ruth and mother. Father and Stephen were up and out of doors in five minutes.

The Roger Marchbanks's stables were blazing. The wind was carrying great red cinders straight over on to the house roofs. The buildings were a little down on our side of the hill, and a thick plantation of evergreens hid them from the town. Everything was still as death but the crackling of the flames. A fire in the country, in the dead of night, to those first awakened to the knowledge of it, is a stealthily fearful, horribly triumphant thing. Not a voice nor a bell smiting the air, where all will soon be outcry and confusion; only the fierce, busy diligence of the blaze, having all its own awful will, and making steadfast headway against the sleeping skill of men.

We all put on some warm things, and went right over. Father found Mr. Marchbanks, with his gardener, at the back of the house, playing upon the scorching frames of the conservatory building with the garden engine. Up on the house-roof two other men-servants were hanging wet carpets from the eaves, and dashing down buckets of water here and there, from the reservoir inside.

Mr. Marchbanks gave father a small red trunk. "Will you take this to your house and keep it safe?" he asked. And father hastened away with it.

Within the house, women were rushing, half dressed, through the rooms, and down the passages and staircases. We went up through the back piazza, and met Mrs. Hobart in her fire-gown at the unfastened door. There was no card to leave this time, no servant to say that Mrs. Marchbanks was "particularly engaged."

Besides her gown, Mrs. Hobart had her theory, all ready for a fire. Just exactly what she should do, first and next, and straight through, in case of such a thing.

She had recited it over to herself and her family till it was so learned by heart that she believed no flurry of the moment would put it wholly out of their heads.

She went straight up Mrs. Marchbanks's great oak stair-case, to go up which had been such a privilege for the bidden few. Rough feet would go over it, unbidden, to night.

She met Mrs. Marchbanks at her bedroom door. In the upper story the cook and house-maids were handing buckets now to the men outside. The fine parlor-maid was down in the kitchen at the force-pump, with Olivia and Adelaide to help and keep her at it. A nursery-girl was trying to wrap up the younger children in all sorts of wrong things, upside down.

"Take these children right over to my house," said Mrs. Hobart. "Barbara Holabird! Come up here!"

"I don't know what to do first," said Mrs. Marchbanks, excitedly. "Mr. Marchbanks has taken away his papers; but there's all the silver — and the pictures — and every-thing! And the house will be full of men directly!" She looked round the room nervously, and went and picked up her braided "chignon" from the dressing-table. Mrs. Marchbanks could "receive" splendidly; she had never thought what she should do at a fire. She knew all the rules of the grammar of life; she had not learned anything about the exceptions.

"Elijah! Come up here!" called Mrs. Hobart again, over the balusters. And Elijah, Mrs. Hobart's Yankee man-servant, brought up on her father's farm, clattered up stairs in his thick boots, that sounded on the smooth oak as if a horse were coming.

Mrs. Marchbanks looked bewilderedly around her room again. "They 'll break everything!" she said, and took down a little Sèvres cup from a bracket.

"There, Mrs. Marchbanks! You just go off with the children. I 'll see to things. Let me have your keys."

"They 're all in my upper bureau-drawer," said Mrs. Marchbanks. "Besides, there is n't much locked, except the silver. I wish Matilda would come." Matilda is Mrs. Lewis Marchbanks. "The children can go there, of course."

"It is too far," said Mrs. Hobart. "Go and make them go to bed in my great front room. Then you 'll feel easier, and can come back. You 'll want Mrs. Lewis Marchbanks's house for the rest of you, and plenty of things besides."

While she was talking she had pulled the blankets and coverlet from the bed, and spread them on the floor. Mrs. Marchbanks actually walked down stairs with her chignon in one hand and the Sèvres cup in the other.

"People *do* do curious things at fires," said Mrs. Hobart, cool, and noticing everything.

She had got the bureau-drawers emptied now into the blankets. Barbara followed her lead, and they took all the clothing from the closets and wardrobe.

"Tie those up, Elijah. Carry them off to a safe place, and come back, up here."

Then she went to the next room. From that to the next and the next, she passed on, in like manner, — Barbara, and by this time the rest of us, helping ; stripping the beds, and making up huge bundles on the floors of the contents of presses, drawers, and boxes.

"Clothes are the first thing," said she. "And this way, you are pretty sure to pick up everything." Everything *was* picked up, from Mrs. Marchbanks's jewel-case and her silk dresses, to Mr. Marchbanks's shaving brushes, and the children's socks that they had had pulled off last night.

Elijah carried them all off, and piled them up in Mrs. Hobart's great clean laundry-room to await orders. The men hailed him as he went and came, to do this, or fetch that. "I 'm doing *one* thing," he answered. "You keep to yourn."

"They 're comin'," he said, as he returned after his third trip. "The bells are ringin', an' they 're a swarmin' up the hill, — two ingines, an' a ruck o' boys an' men. Melindy, she 's keepin' the laundry door locked, an' a lettin' on me in."

Mrs. Marchbanks came hurrying back before the crowd. Some common, ecstatic little boys, rushing foremost to the fire, hustled her on her own lawn. She could hardly believe even yet in this inevitable irruption of the Great Uninvited.

Mrs. Lewis Marchbanks and Maud met her and came in with her. Mr. Marchbanks and Arthur had hastened round to the rear, where the other gentlemen were still hard at work.

"Now," said Mrs. Hobart, as lightly and cheerily as if it had been the putting together of a Christmas pudding, and she were ready for the citron or the raisins, — " now — all that beautiful china ! "

She had been here at one great, general party, and remembered the china ; although her party-call, like all her others, had been a failure. Mrs. Marchbanks received a good many people in a grand, occasional, wholesale civility, to whom she would not sacrifice any fraction of her private hours.

Mrs. Hobart found **her** way by instinct to the china-closet, — **the china-room,** more properly speaking. Mrs. Marchbanks rather followed than led.

The shelves, laden with costly pottery, reached from floor **to** ceiling. The polish and the colors flashed already **in the** fierce light of the closely neighboring flames. **Great** drifts and clouds **of smoke** against the windows were urging **in** and stifling **the air.** The first rush **of** water from the engines beat against the walls.

"We must work awful quick now," said Mrs. Hobart. "**But** keep cool. We ain't afire yet."

She gave **Mrs. Marchbanks her own** keys, which she had brought down stairs. That lady opened her safe and took out her silver, which Arthur Marchbanks and James Hobart received from her and carried away.

Mrs. Hobart herself went up the step-ladder that stood there before the shelves, and began to hand down piles of plates, and heavy single pieces. "**Keep** folks out, Elijah," **she ordered to** her man.

We all helped. There were a good many of us by this **time,** — Olivia, **and** Adelaide, **and** the servant-girls released from below, besides the other Marchbankses, and the Hobarts, and people who came in, until Elijah stopped them. He shut the heavy walnut doors that led from drawing-room and library to the hall, and turned the great keys in their polished locks. Then he stood by the garden entrance in the sheltered side-angle, through which **we** passed with our burdens, **and** defended **that** against invasion. There **was now** such an absolute order among ourselves that **the** moral **force** of it repressed the **excitement without** that might **else have** rushed **in and** overborne us.

"**You jest keep** back; **it's all** right **here,**" Elijah would say, deliberately **and** authoritatively, holding **the** door against unlicensed comers; and boys and men stood back **as they** might have done outside **the** shine and splendor **and** privilege **of an** entertainment.

It lasted till we got **well** through; **till** we had gone, **one by one,** down the field, across **to our** house, the short **way, back** and forth, leaving the china, pile after pile, **safe in our** cellar-kitchen.

Meanwhile, without **our** thinking **of it,** Barbara had **been locked out** upon the **stairs.** Mother had found a tall Fayal **clothes-basket, and had** collected **in it,** carefully, little pictures and precious things that could be easily moved, and might **be** as easily **lost** or destoyed. Barbara mounted guard **over this, watching** for **a right** person to whom **to** deliver it.

Standing there, like Casabianca, rough men rushed by her to get up to the roof. The hall was filling with a crowd, mostly of the curious, untrustworthy sort, for **the** work just then lay elsewhere.

So Barbara held by, only drawing back with the **basket,** into an angle of the wide landing. **N**obody must seize it heedlessly; things **were** only laid in lightly, for careful handling. **In it were** children's photographs, taken **in** days that they had grown away from; little treasures of art and remembrance, picked **up** in foreign **travel, or**

gifts of friends ; all sorts of priceless odds and ends that
people have about a house, never thinking what would
become of them in a night like this. So Barbara stood
by.

Suddenly somebody, just come, and springing in at the
open door, heard his name.

"Harry ! Help me with this !" And Harry Goldthwaite pushed aside two men at the foot of the staircase,
lifted up a small boy and swung him over the baluster,
and ran up to the landing.

"Take hold of it with me," said Barbara, hurriedly.
"It is valuable. We must carry it ourselves. Don't let
anybody touch it. Over to Mrs. Hobart's."

"Hendee !" called out Harry to Mark Hendee, who
appeared below. "Keep those people off, will you?
Make way !" And so they two took the big basket
steadily by the ears, and went away with it together.
The first we knew about it was when, on their way back,
they came down upon our line of march toward Elijah's
door.

Beyond this, there was uo order to chronicle. So far,
it seems longer in the telling than it did in the doing.
We had to work "awful quick," as Mrs. Hobart said.
But the nice and hazardous work was all done. Even
the press that held the table-napery was emptied to the
last napkin, and all was safe.

Now the hall doors were thrown open ; wagons were
driven up to the entrances, and loaded with everything
that came first, as things are ordinarily " saved " at a
fire. These were taken over to Mrs. Lewis Marchbanks's.
Books and pictures, furniture, bedding, carpets ; quanti-

ties were carried away, and quantities were piled up on the lawn. The men-servants came and looked after these; they had done all they could elsewhere; they left the work to the firemen now, and there was little hope of saving the house. The window-frames were smoking, and the panes were cracking with the heat, and fire was running along the piazza roofs before we left the building. The water was giving out.

After that we had to stand and see it burn. The wells and cisterns were dry, and the engines stood helpless.

The stable roofs fell in with a crash, and the flames reared up as from a great red crater and whirlpool of fire. They lashed forth and seized upon charred walls and timbers that were ready, without their touch, to spring into live combustion. The whole southwest front of the mansion was overswept with almost instant sheets of fire. Fire poured in at the casements; through the wide, airy halls; up and into the rooms where we had stood a little while before; where, a little before that, the children had been safe asleep in their nursery beds.

Mrs. Marchbanks, like any other burnt-out woman, had gone to the home that offered to her, — her sister-in-law's; Olivia and Adelaide were going to the Haddens; the children were at Mrs. Hobart's; the things that, in their rich and beautiful arrangement, had made *home*, as well as enshrined the Marchbanks family in their sacredness of elegance, were only miscellaneous "loads" now, transported and discharged in haste, or heaped up confusedly to await removal. And the sleek servants, to whom, doubtless, it had seemed that their Rome could never fall, were suddenly, as much as any common Bridgets and Patricks, "out of a place."

Not that there would be any permanent difference; it was only the story and attitude of a night. The power was still behind; the " Tailor " would sew things over again directly. Mrs. Roger Marchbanks would be comparatively composed and in order, at Mrs. Lewis's, in a few days, — receiving her friends, who would hurry to make " fire-calls," as they would to make party or engagement or other special occasion visits; the cordons would be stretched again; not one of the crowd of people who went freely in and out of her burning rooms that night, and worked hardest, saving her library and her pictures and her carpets, would come up in cool blood and ring her door-bell now; the sanctity and the dignity would be as unprofanable as ever.

It was about four in the morning — the fire still burning — when Mrs. Holabird went round upon the outskirts of the groups of lookers-on, to find and gather together her own flock. Rosamond and Ruth stood in a safe corner with the Haddens. Where was Barbara?

Down against the close trunks of a cluster of linden-trees had been thrown cushions and carpets and some bundles of heavy curtains, and the like. Coming up behind, Mrs. Holabird saw, sitting upon this heap, two persons. She knew Barbara's hat, with its white gull's breast; but somebody had wrapped her up in a great crimson table-cover, with a bullion fringe. Somebody was Harry Goldthwaite, sitting there beside her; Barbara, with only her head visible, was behaving, out here in this unconventional place and time, with a tranquillity and composure which of late had been apparently impossible to her in parlors.

"What will Mrs. Marchbanks do with Mrs. Hobart after this, I wonder?" Mrs. Holabird heard Harry say.

"She'll give her a sort of brevet," replied Barbara. "For gallant and meritorious services. It will be, 'Our friend Mrs. Hobart; a near neighbor of ours; she was with us all that terrible night of the fire, you know." It will be a great honor; but it won't be a full commission."

Harry laughed.

"Queer things happen when you are with us," said Barbara. "First, there was the whirlwind, last year, — and now the fire."

14

" After the whirlwind and the fire — " said Harry.

" I was n't thinking of the Old Testament," interrupted Barbara.

" Came a still, small voice," persisted Harry. " If
I 'm wicked, Barbara, I can't help it.   You put it into my
head."

" I don't see any wickedness," answered Barbara,
quickly. " That was the voice of the Lord. I suppose
it is always coming."

" Then, Barbara — "

Then Mrs. Holabird walked away again.

The next day — *that* day, after our eleven o'clock
breakfast — Harry came back, and was at Westover all
day long.

Barbara got up into mother's room at evening, alone
with her.   She brought a cricket, and came and sat down
beside her, and put her cheek upon her knee.

" Mother," she said, softly, " I don't see but you 'll
have to get me ready, and let me go."

" My dear child !   When ?   What do you mean ? "

" Right off.   Harry is under orders, you know.   And
they may hardly ever be so nice again.   And — if we *are*
going through the world together — might n't we as well
begin to go ? "

" Why, Barbara, you take my breath away !   But
then you always do !   What is it ? "

" It 's the Katahdin, fitting out at New York to join
the European squadron.   Commander Shapleigh is a
great friend of Harry's ; his wife and daughter are in
New York, going out, by Southampton steamer, when
the frigate leaves, to meet him there.   They would take

me, he says; and — that's what Harry wants, mother. There'll be a little while first, — as much, perhaps, as we should ever have."

"Barbara, my darling! But you've nothing ready!"

"No, I suppose not. I never do have. Everything is an emergency with me; but I always emerge! I can get things in London," she added. "Everybody does."

The end of it was that Mrs. Holabird had to catch her breath again, as mothers do; and that Barbara is getting ready to be married just as she does everything else.

Rose has some nice things — laid away, new; she always has; and mother has unsuspected treasures; and we all had new silk dresses for Leslie's wedding, and Ruth had a bright idea about that.

"I'm as tall as either of you, now," she said; "and we girls are all of a size, as near as can be, mother and all; and we'll just wear the dresses once more, you see, and then put them right into Barbara's trunk. They'll be all the bonnier and luckier for her, I know. We can get others any time."

We laughed at her at first; but we came round afterward to think that it was a good plan. Rosamond's silk was a lovely violet, and Ruth's was blue; Barbara's own was pearly gray; we were glad, now, that no two of us had dressed alike. The violet and the gray had been chosen because of our having worn quiet black-and-white all summer for grandfather. We had never worn crape; or what is called "deep" mourning. "You shall never do that," said mother, "till the deep mourning comes. Then you will choose for yourselves."

We have had more time than we expected. There has

been some beautiful **delay or other about** machinery, —
the Katahdin's, **that** is ; **and** Commander Shapleigh **has
been** ever **so** kind.   **Harry has been back** and **forth to
New** York **two or three** times.   Once **he took** Stephen
with him ; Steve **stayed at** Uncle John's ; but **he was down**
at the **yard, and on board ships, and** got acquainted with
some **midshipmen ; and he** has quite made up his mind to
try to get in at the Naval Academy as **soon as he is old
enough,** and **to be** a navy officer himself.

We are comfortable **at** home ; not hurried after all.
We are determined **not to be** ; **last days are too** precious.

"**Don't let 's be all** taken **up with** ' **things,'** " says Barbara.   "**I can** *buy* ' **things** ' any time.   But now, — I
want you ! "

Aunt Roderick's **present helped** wonderfully.   It was
magnanimous of her; it was coals of fire.   **We** should
have believed she **was** inspired, — **or** possessed, — but
that Ruth went down **to** Boston with her.

There came home, in a box, two days after, from **Jordan**
and Marsh's, the loveliest " suit," all made and finished,
of brown **poplin.   To** think **of Aunt** Roderick's getting
anything *made*, at an " establishment " !   But Ruth **says**
she put her principles into her unpickable pocket, and just
took her porte-monnaie in her hand.

Bracelets and pocket-handkerchiefs **have** come from
New York ; all **the** " girls " **here in** Westover have given
presents **of** ornaments, or little things to wear ; they know
there **is no** housekeeping **to** provide for.   Barbara says
her trousseau " flies together " ; she just has to sit and **look**
at it.

She has begged that old garnet **and white silk, though,**

at last, from mother. Ruth saw her fold it up and put it, the very first thing, into the bottom of her new trunk. She patted it down gently, and gave it a little stroke, just as she pats and strokes mother herself sometimes.

"*All* new things are only dreary," she says. "I must have some of the old."

"I should just like to know one thing, — if I might," said Rosamond, deferentially, after we had begun to go to bed one evening. She was sitting in her white night-dress, on the box-sofa, with her shoe in her hand. "I should just like to know what made you behave so before-hand, Barbara?"

"I was in a buzz," said Barbara. "And it *was* before-hand. I suppose I knew it was coming, — like a thunder-storm."

"You came pretty near securing that it *should n't* come," said Rosamond, "after all."

"I could n't help that; it was n't my part of the affair."

"You might have just kept quiet, as you were before," said Rose.

"Wait and see," said Barbara, concisely. "People should n't come bringing things in their hands. It 's just like going down stairs to get these presents. The very minute I see a corner of one of those white paper parcels, don't I begin to look every way, and say all sorts of things in a hurry? Would n't I like to turn my back and run off if I could? Why don't they put them under the sofa, or behind the door, I wonder?"

"After all —" began Rosamond, still with the question-ing inflection.

"After all —" said Barbara, "there was the fire. That, luckily, was something else!"

"Does there always have to be a fire?" asked Ruth, laughing.

"Wait and see," repeated Barbara. "Perhaps you'll have an earthquake."

We have time for talks. We take up every little chink of time to have each other in. We want each other in all sorts of ways; we never wanted each other so, or *had* each other so, before.

Delia Waite is here, and there is some needful stitching going on; but the minutes are alongside the stitches; they are not eaten up; there are minutes everywhere. We have got a great deal of life into a little while; and — we have finished up our Home Story, to the very present instant.

Who finishes it? Who tells it?

Well, — "the kettle began it." Mrs. Peerybingle — pretty much — finished it. That is, the story began itself, then Ruth discovered that it was beginning, and began, first, to put it down. Then Ruth grew busy, and she would n't always have told quite enough of the Ruthy part; and Mrs. Holabird got hold of it, as she gets hold of everything, and she would not let it suffer a " solution of continuity." Then, partly, she observed; and partly we told tales, and recollected and reminded; and partly, here and there, we rushed in, — especially I, Barbara, — and did little bits ourselves; and so it came to be a " Song o' Sixpence," and at least four Holabirds were " singing in the pie."

Do you think it is — sarcastically — a " pretty dish to set before the king"? Have we shown up our friends and neighbors too plainly ?   There is one comfort ; nobody knows exactly where " Z——" is ; and there are friends and neighbors everywhere.

I am sure nobody can complain, if I don't.   This last part—the Barbarous part—is a continual breach of confidence.   I have a great mind, now, not to respect anything myself; not even that cadet button, made into a pin, which Ruth wears so shyly.   To be sure, Mrs. Hautayne has one too ; she and Ruth are the only two girls whom Dakie Thayne considers *worth* a button ; but Leslie is an old, old friend ; older than Dakie in years, so that it could never have been like Ruth with her ; and she never was a bit shy about it either.   Besides—

Well, you cannot have any more than there is.   The story is told as far as we—or anybody—has gone.   You must let the world go round the sun again, a time or two ; everything has not come to pass yet—even with " We Girls."

THE END.